SHARING SNOW

DARK AND TWISTED FAIRY TALES

ANDIE M. LONG

This book is a work of fiction. Names, characters, places, and incidents are either the product of the author's imagination or are used fictitiously, and any resemblance to actual persons, living or dead, events or locales is entirely coincidental.

No part of this book may be reproduced or transmitted in any form or by any means, electronic or mechanical, including photocopying, recording or by any information storage and retrieval system without the written permission of the author, except for the use of brief quotations in a book review.

The author, Andie M. Long, does not consent to any Artificial Intelligence (AI), generative AI, large language model, machine learning, chatbot, or other automated analysis, generative process, or replication programme to reproduce, mimic, remix, summarise, or otherwise replicate any part of this creative work, via any means.

The author supports the right of humans to control their artistic works. No part of this book has been created using AI-generated images or narrative, as known by the author.

Copyright © 2023 by Andie M. Long.
All rights reserved.
Cover design by Art Lynx
Formatting by Angel Alley Designs

Trigger Warnings

Author note

It's very hard to know what might trigger someone while reading. For me I can't read about anyone suffering with cancer.

However, with these dark and twisted fairy tales, I have decided to add a list of themes for those who need them as these books push boundaries I rarely go beyond in my writing.

My deepest darkest seeking readers can move swiftly on.
Andie xo

This book includes

Craving pain to the point of seeking someone to cause this by punching/hitting (in the context of supernatural beings, not humans).

Sexual assault.
Other violence.
Kidnapping.
Casual sex and multiple partners.

Because sometimes we need to let our dark side show.

Summary

A paranormal fairy tale re-telling... of a vampire, seven wolf shifters, and a shared love.

They said that Once Upon a Time an evil queen looked in a mirror and found she was no longer the fairest of them all.

But what if a vision, this time appearing in a crystal ball was of a wolf's fated mate? A beautiful female vampire called Snow? What if the wolf had sworn vengeance on her kind after the murder of his father?

After Snow walks into pack territory uninvited, Alpha Kellan locks her in his cabin. But can he fight his attraction to his new prisoner, while dealing with the other wolf pack males who want her too?

This is the second book in Andie M. Long's dark and twisted fairy tale re-tellings. Wicked words with happy forever afters.

Chapter 1
Ella

The snow outside was a welcome distraction as I gave birth to my first-born child. Flakes dashed against the windowpane, some singly, some in a cluster as the wind outside buffeted them against the glass.

Tap, tap, tap, it went and then the wind would howl once more as it caught its next flurry.

My husband paced the length of our bedroom while ever the midwife checked me over. Usually, so cool, calm, and collected, Beau was currently anything but. The man who couldn't wait to get me with child was now a nervous wreck.

His footsteps tapped against the floor.

The snow tapped against the window.

The clock ticked on as the hours passed.

"I think you can begin pushing now, Mrs Salinger. Next contraction, okay?"

I nodded.

Beau was standing at the window once more. As the snowflakes stuck there like spiders clinging onto a destroyed web, I remembered how unique a snowflake was, how beautiful, and as my daughter was born, I instantly knew her name.

Snow.

The pain seized me, and I began the journey that led to my daughter's appearance. Beau, by my side, held my hand and whispered words of encouragement and reassurance. But I wasn't really listening. I was focused on the final efforts that would make me a mother.

And then she was here. A short cry announcing her arrival.

The midwife quickly checked her over and pronounced our daughter a picture of health. She passed her to me along with her congratulations. I drank in every bit of my beautiful baby. This surreal feeling of the flesh of a newborn against my own chest. Her cold skin against mine.

The short smattering of hair atop her head was black as a crow's feathers and her skin was as pale as a vampire's should be. I smoothed my fingers over her hair, delighting in the feel of it. So soft and so very real. She was here! I clutched her towards me, our first embrace.

Beau looked down at us both, his expression one of both of awe and pride. I knew this exact expression would be mirrored in my own.

"Our beautiful daughter. We are parents, Ella!"

"I wish to call her Snow," I told him. I pointed to the window. "The snowflakes are beautiful and unique."

He looked at her again now apprised of this information. "Snow Salinger. That sounds perfect," he replied. "And you are, little daughter of mine. Just utterly perfect."

My heart was so full, I was surprised my chest didn't explode.

"Hello, little Snow," I said softly. "I'm your mummy and this is your daddy." Beau and I shared a moment before gazing back down at our newborn baby.

There was such love in the room in that moment.

It didn't take long however before the memories of the past emerged. I pictured my own parents looking down at me after my birth. While I knew my mother would have gazed at me in love, my father's expression was the one I thought about, because years later he threw out my mother and imprisoned me in the basement of what had been the family home. If my father had looked at me with joy after my arrival, it would have only been as a celebration of the fact he was one step closer to stealing mum's family's business.

"Don't do that, darling," Beau whispered as he stroked a finger down our baby's cheek. Of course he'd read my mind, my guards lowered in my stripped-down birth state. "I am not your father, and Snow is the most precious gift I have ever received."

Snow made a snuffling motion and I looked to the midwife.

"She's ready for a feed. Let me just get you the bottle."

I nodded.

In times gone by, the mother would have slit her wrist and held it to her baby's mouth. These days though were more civilised, and I'd prepared a bottle in advance.

Snow rooted towards the teat the moment it went near her perfect rosebud pout. Latching on, she began to drink and as she did so, her pale cheeks bloomed red.

I had a mother's bias, but I also knew beauty when I saw it and Snow Salinger was captivating.

The years passed, and as Snow's age increased so did our family. A perfect elder child, she helped me with the smaller children even if not asked. She was a natural organiser, telling her younger siblings what they needed to do, and they all looked up to her with worship in their eyes.

Yet there was always a restlessness to our eldest daughter. Despite being surrounded with love and reassured of her safety, at times I would catch her worrying her lip, as if the weight of the world rested on her shoulders. Then she'd meet my gaze and smile and I'd think I must have imagined it.

Now, it was the eve of her twentieth birthday, and we all gathered in the living room ready to celebrate as the clock struck twelve.

Snow stood by the window staring out. Just like when she'd been born all those years ago, snow once again fell, although this time it settled on the ground, no wind swirling it in a maelstrom.

No, I felt the maelstrom was inside our daughter, waiting to escape. This most exquisite woman, my darling daughter, met my gaze with those dark brown eyes of hers and her lips parted as if about to confess something.

But as the clock began its chimes and Beau began

the countdown with the rest of the family joining in, her words were swallowed back down.

The celebrations began in earnest, but this year I didn't feel the same contentment I'd enjoyed every year before.

This time in the pit of my stomach I felt dread.

Chapter 2

Snow

The fist hit my jaw, making my head snap back. My teeth bit through my tongue and I spat out a mouthful of blood.

Andre's eyes flashed with red mist satisfaction as the scent of my blood hit his nose.

His second of smugness became his downfall as I swung my leg and kicked him straight in the balls. Then as he folded in pain, I brought my knee back around and up into his face, the snap of bone and flush of red spray indicating I'd broken his nose.

Fury fought his pain and won, and he advanced on me, but instead of fear I felt a frisson of excitement. Here it came. I pretended to dodge his next punch even though I knew it was a set-up, that he intended to come in from the right. He yanked me by the hair and threw me. My body sailed through the air like I weighed only the same as a paper aeroplane and yet as I hit the wall at the other side plaster detached and fell. The skin on my face scraped against the rough brick all the way down, burning as it destroyed the flesh.

I closed my eyes and inhaled.

The pain.

The burn.

The utter satisfaction of it all.

My pants were damp with how much it turned me on.

Another thing Andre scented.

He swept to my side.

"Want to get out of here?" he asked, with the raise of a brow and a cadence of lust. It wasn't the first time he'd made such an offer. But I wasn't here for his dick. I was here to be destroyed.

I answered with a smug smile.

"Have I tired you out? You think after that amateur performance I should sit on your cock?"

"So you deny me again?" he pondered. "One day you will be in my bed. All this play just makes the wait all the sweeter, little ice queen."

I wanted more. My injuries were already healing, as were Andre's; the dried blood on his face the only reminder that anything untoward had taken place. But

I knew it wasn't going to happen. Not tonight. Andre had given me some of what I needed, and I hadn't returned the favour. His patience with me would be wearing thin.

I didn't want him that way though.

It would be oh so easy to let Andre fuck me raw while I begged for him to hurt me before he pleased me. But always the guilt got in the way of me trying it.

My mother's words of how she met my father.

Her first, her last, her everything… her one, true love.

Four years earlier, I had begun dating a boy at school called Merit. Teenage vampire girls were not immune to crushes and I'd been besotted. My mother had pulled me to one side 'for a chat' after she'd received word from school that my grades were plummeting and my attention to my studies waning.

"Don't rush into a relationship, Snow," she'd warned me. *"We're vampires. We have all the time in the world. Remember, your father sent me away to experience life before letting me commit to a future with him."*

I'd sighed, in the derogatory way of the teenage

years. "Yet you returned and wanted only him, so wasn't that just a waste of time you could have spent together?' I'd asked.

"Maybe. But this way I knew for sure. No one else measured up to your father for me. He was my everything."

I'd rolled my eyes. 'Well, I think it was a pretty dangerous game for Dad to send you out into the bed of others, hoping you'd return. It could have gone very wrong if you'd fallen in love with someone else. You see, Mum, I don't believe in one true love."

She'd gasped at my words, as if I'd announced I'd committed a serious crime.

"How can you see me and your father and not believe?" she'd queried.

"Because I've witnessed people lose a loved one and then find another," I'd explained. "That's why although I understand Dad's reasoning, it still could have proved a disaster, because it's entirely possible to love multiple people at once. You don't only love one of your children, do you?"

Mum had gazed at me then as she did often, like I was a thing of pure wonder. She reached out and stroked her fingertips down my cheek.

"My wise daughter. I thought I would teach you all about the world, but sometimes you teach me. Perhaps

fate was what reunited your father and I, or luck on his part." She'd smiled.

"I know one other thing," I'd said.

"Yes?"

"If you had fallen in love with anyone else, Dad would have come and stolen you away anyhow."

We'd laughed then, before my mother had made me agree to see Merit less and to study more. She needn't have worried. My interest in him waned quickly. I lost my virginity to him but found sex didn't satisfy me in the way I'd hoped. It didn't assuage my hunger, even when we shared the bite. No, it was after a teenaged temper tantrum, when I'd returned to my bedroom and thrown myself repeatedly at a wall that I'd realised what I did like.

Pain.

Feeling the overwhelming sensations and then the healing that came after for a vampire righted me somehow. I'd feel out of sorts and then after a fight, I'd feel like I'd been reassembled in the correct way for a while.

Though the satisfaction didn't last for long.

I craved pain more than I craved blood.

What scared me was I still wasn't fully receiving everything I needed.

So what came next?

I left Andre and returned home to get ready. He was unaware but the following day was my birthday, and my family were throwing me a party. My parents thought I'd gone out to buy a new dress for the occasion, so I made sure to pop in a store on my way home and quickly purchase an outfit. I chose what to others may have looked kooky, but to me appealed to my love of colour: a dress with a lemon silk skirt, and a blue corset bodice with short, puff sleeves. The bodice was threaded with a long red lace, and I'd purchased a red hair ribbon and shoes to complete the look.

There was a knock at the door.

"Yes?"

It opened and my mum popped her head through. "Are you almost ready?"

"Yes, I'll walk downstairs with you," I said, from my seat in front of the dressing table. I brushed my hair one last time and fixed my ribbon in place before rising.

"Oh, Snow, you look so very beautiful," Mum said, placing a hand to her mouth. I saw the blush of rose-coloured water at her lower eyelids as I stood next to her. "That dress would work on no-one but you," she added with a hint of amusement. "Always so different."

She didn't know how true her words were, and I wondered if now—as my twenties approached—it was time to confide about just how different I was.

Leaving the room together, I looked at the family photos mum had hung on the walls. Our smiling faces on the colourful pictures were just one of the ways she'd attempted to modernise Moonstone castle over the years, but the place always seemed to cling to its gothic splendour, especially when the sun set, and the rooms were cast in shadow.

"Is she coming down anytime soon? I'm bored," whined one of my brothers from the bottom of the stairs. Mum and I laughed at Reid's typical teenage whining and picked up our pace to join the party.

It was a simple celebration as always. My mother and father, my five siblings, and our godmother Iris. Music played and there was a buffet of party food, even though none of us needed to eat. I chatted with everyone, playing the role of the birthday girl, and then I noticed it had begun to snow. Standing by the window looking out, I recalled my mum's words of how she'd decided my name.

How beautiful.

How unique.

I knew I was considered pretty, but if anything, it made me uncomfortable. It was all I'd ever heard. Strangers had stopped my parents in the street to comment about my appearance. Had got in my personal space and touched my hair or my cheek. Coupled with my parents' overprotection, it had led to me keeping close to their side if I went out as a child. Made me fearful of contact.

Then I'd become a teenager, my breasts and hips growing, and it became even more difficult to avoid the lustful looks or the envious ones. So many people never bothering with the fact I was well educated and liked to debate current affairs. I'd seek out my father if I ever had questions on general knowledge. It became our thing, time spent debating subjects affecting the world. I wanted an understanding of the world beyond vampires, and as we lived mainly around humans, I became captivated by human psychology.

Some humans developed such uncomfortableness with their bodies that they would amputate a limb. It was called body integrity identity disorder. I wondered if my anger about being noticed for my prettiness was another reason I liked to smash my face into walls, or have Andre punch it. Being a vampire I was healed more or less immediately. No one aware of my secret fighting or the urge for violence that ran beneath the surface. It wasn't that I hated my looks. It was the frustration inside me that needed to be released. To escape, to experience more. But it tormented me that being given a perfect upbringing with a loving family set off something inside me that wanted to know the depths of darkness. I sought balance maybe? We were vampires, fed blood via bottles and living a human-like existence. I felt my body was a cage and my inner animal needed to be let loose.

Looking at the window, I'd wished it were open. I might have assumed my bat shape and escaped.

Feeling my mum's gaze on me, I met her eyes. It was time for me to tell her how I felt about everything. About all the feelings that whirled inside me, then I could ask for her guidance in quietening them. I opened my mouth to speak...

But the countdown to midnight started and everyone joined in, so I pushed it all aside, ready to carry on with the act.

"My present first!" Reid insisted. Not because he was excitable, but because he wanted to get out of here as fast as possible and back to his PlayStation.

I opened the parcel, revealing a pair of fluffy socks. He stood up, already taller than I despite only being fifteen and he ruffled the top of my head, dislodging my ribbon. "Happy birthday!" he said, then off he went, walking towards the door, only to be called back by our father and scolded for trying to leave the family get-together.

Gene pulled open my ribbon and tied it around his own head, ever the joker. "Does it suit me?" he asked, before doing an impersonation. "I am the prettiest of them all," he teased, before adding, "Men follow me around like panting dogs."

"Hush, Gene, before your father goes feral," Mum said, laughing. He passed me his gift which was an assortment of hair accessories.

Phillipe was next. I unwrapped a journal and a pen. The journal said *My Private Confessions* on it and was fitted with a lock. As he fixed me with a look, I got the impression my seventeen-year-old brother might know more about me than I desired. I felt my shoulders knot. "Thank you," I said. He nodded and walked away.

Iris insisted on going next. She'd made me a beautiful three-piece trouser suit. There was a strappy camisole, some leggings, and a fitted jacket. It was black with a silver sparkle to it and would make me look a gothic queen. "I know you love your bright colours, but I just know this will look sensational on you," she said. I kissed her in thanks.

Then it was my sisters' turn. Isabel handed me a pile of what were clearly wrapped books, six in total. She was a total bookworm, and I had no doubt she'd have selected these carefully based on what she knew of my interests. I quickly cast my eyes over them and thanked her. Dove had bought me bath and shower products and we laughed as Mum rolled her eyes. There was a line of products under a brand called *Dove*, and that was what she'd got me. An in-joke she did with everyone.

Finally, it was time for my parents to reveal their gift to me.

"We have to go outside," Mum said.

"But it's snowing," Isabel whined.

"Don't be such a pussy," Gene teased, earning a warning raised brow from Dad.

Just outside the back door, under the porch, was an electric bike with a huge red bow on it, reminding me of the hair ribbon Gene still had on his head. I leaned over and took it back off him and placed it back on my own head. Then I stepped towards the bike.

"I love it," I enthused, breaking out in a huge smile.

"Just please be careful of tree roots etc if you cut through the woods," Dad warned.

"I will."

"Give it a test drive then," Dove encouraged.

I pulled off the bow and hunched up my dress to climb upon the bike.

"Maybe this wasn't the best idea, given she's in a party outfit. What if she falls and impales herself on a branch because her legs get tangled?" Mum worried, but I was off. I drove up and down the front of the house as the snow landed on my face, and I imagined setting off down the driveway. But in my imagination, I was in bare feet, the pebbled driveway shredding the skin of my soles, while the wind sailed through my hair and the ice-cold snowflakes dashed at my skin before falling to cover over the blood-stained tracks I left in my wake.

"Snow, that's enough now. It'll still be there tomorrow," Mum urged, the concern winning over just letting me have fun on my birthday. She saw peril that wasn't there. There wasn't a single branch or even a stick on the drive. Just a faint smattering of fallen snow. However, I cycled back to the porch where my Dad lifted me off the bike. I embraced everyone again with my thanks for all my birthday gifts and we carried on celebrating for another hour or so.

Finally, back in my room, poring over my gifts, I felt happiness as I recalled the love of my family. How lucky I was that we were so close. How fortunate to have both my parents here with me, still so in love; and siblings that were friends as well as kin. But as dawn broke and sleep claimed me, I dreamed of flinging open the castle doors and running to an unknown destination.

Chapter 3

Kellan

We were gathered in the boardroom to discuss ongoing pack business. I'd been the alpha only a month, but I'd been prepared for the role all my damn life.

Just ten minutes in and Trent barged into the room, the doors flying apart and hitting the walls. One look at his hands and I knew why.

He carried a box.

A black cardboard box tied with a red ribbon. Trent placed the box down on the table and stood there, his hands trembling either with rage or fear. I looked up to meet his eyes.

Fear.

This was the third box now, and I would act the same as when the first two arrived—indifferent.

"Do you w-want me to open it?" Trent asked, his hands hovering over the elaborately tied bow. His nerves weren't only for the potential content. He was also bracing himself for my reaction.

"No. I want you to sit your fucking arse down in your chair where I'm in the middle of discussing pack business. That shit can wait," I scolded.

"But—"

"Sit down," I yelled, with a roar. Trent raced to his seat, his eyes meeting those of a few other of the pack council.

I knew what they thought. That I was in denial. But I wasn't. I just had large boots to fill, and at this time a weakened pack would be a disaster. More than ever we needed to stay as one, an elite team ready to defend ourselves from attack.

"Cast your eyes on the papers in front of you. This is the new security plan. One of the council will monitor the woods at all times, two over the evening when the woods are empty of most of the pack. This will be done mainly by infra-red camera security, but there will also be patrols. We need to know how these boxes are getting in the delivery vans."

"It would be a lot easier if we knew our enemy," Diego said, with a sigh.

"Our enemy is a vampire. That's all we need to

know," I snapped. "They've always been our enemy, but for the last century have not been stupid enough to trespass on our territory. One has now made a move and we will respond. This is your priority above anything else, understand?"

My other six members of the council—brothers to me in every way other than blood—nodded their heads.

"When we attack, we will make sure it only needs to happen the once. A clear indication that we do not play the teasing prey games of the cold ones. After which no one will dare threaten us again for many more centuries." I looked around at them all. "You know what you need to do now. Pierce, as head of security, please advise the others as necessary. And remember, we work hard before we play hard. That's how we survive. Okay, I declare this meeting over."

Tommo rose. "Come on. Let's get working hard so that later we can play hard," he encouraged the others.

They didn't need any more encouragement than that and left the room. I stood up and walked over to the box.

My hands went either side of the ribbon, and I pulled, watching the bow untie and the ribbon fall onto the table. Then I lifted the lid off the box and peered inside, seeing the heart. There was no blood.

That was part of the message as to where it had come from. First had been his head, second had been his hands. But never any blood.

Because they would have drunk that. Whoever *they* were.

I picked up the note.

Piece by piece
　I'll return him to you
　The ruination of my life
　Your only clue
　I abide by the words:
　Do unto others
　As they have done to you.

It was the same note as in the previous two boxes.

While opening the box, I'd heard the door open behind me. I knew who it would be.

"What is it this time?" my stepmother Nala asked, placing a hand on my arm.

I flinched at her touch, and her proximity. I didn't do feelings, just business.

Picking up the box, I thrust it into her arms. "Put it with the rest. Eventually, we'll be able to bury him."

She looked inside and her eyes filled with tears before she gathered herself, nostrils flaring. "They will rue the day they killed your father," she ground out.

"Your feelings will get you killed," I snapped. "Better you learn more self-defence than torture yourself repeatedly. He's gone. Staring at his body parts won't bring him back."

"I'd rather die having loved, than to simply exist," she retorted. "Otherwise, what's the point?"

But I was halfway out the door as she uttered her words, on my way to the gym to push my body to its limits.

The truth was Nala had been free to love. As alpha of the pack, and son of the alpha before that, I was not. Love distracted you and made you weak, to your enemy's advantage.

Sweat ran down my back in rivulets as I squatted and raised the bar over my head one more time.

"I bet you could lift me above your head like a feather," a female voice uttered from behind me. I recognised the modulation of her tone. What she felt was sultry and seductive was to me like fingernails down a blackboard.

I lowered the bar slowly back to the floor. "We'll never find out, Raina," I said simply, meeting her gaze in her mirrored reflection and seeing her pout.

"A girl can but hope," she added softly, flicking a blonde ringlet.

"Stick to my pack brothers, I'm not available," I told her.

"But that's why I want you," she said, sidling up closer to me. "I always want what I can't have." She slid a hand around my waist.

I grabbed the wrist of that hand, steered her back to the weight equipment and moved her hand atop a dumbbell. "The only things you get to put your hands on here are the weights. Are we clear?"

Raina no longer looked as confident.

"I'm sorry," she said, looking at the floor. "I forgot my place. I won't do it again."

"You're an attractive woman, Raina," I said, making her eyes flicker with optimism. "But I'm not interested."

She visibly slumped.

"My energies are invested in the safety and survival of this pack. One day I will mate bond, and until that day, if I need to fuck, I'll find someone outside of the pack."

"Message received loud and clear," she said,

selecting two weights. "I'll just have to hope that when the time is right, your body will recognise me as a worthy mate."

She just didn't quit. I needed to get out of here and decided instead to go for a run. No one seemed to understand the severity of our situation. Our alpha had been caught and dismembered by an unknown assailant who clearly bore a grudge. It was now my job to keep everyone safe, and yet I couldn't train without being hit on. Raina didn't even want me. Not really. She just wanted to be the alpha's wife and able to act like she was above everyone else. I hoped to God that when my mate bond did hit, it chose someone with independent thought and interests. Someone who didn't feel they needed my approval in order to feel worthy. A wolf wanted a challenge, a chase. An alpha wolf wanted an equal, but one who knew to defer when necessary for the good of the pack, and when to whip a wolf's arse when they were talking out of it. They'd be my partner in pack duties and in play. Raina was not that person. Not yet anyway.

Having left the building, I took off through the woods. Our woodland was vast and went on for miles, with dirt tracks made for vehicle access. The edges of the woods were fenced off and had locked security gates. Despite security cameras monitoring the area, so far, the mystery assailant had somehow thrown the three boxes received to date onto the back of other trailers brought into the compound, the drivers having no clue how they'd got there. The boxes had my name and address typed on a label stuck to the top of the box.

Another clue it was a vampire. They could have used compulsion to wipe the drivers' memories of them.

I ran until I felt like my lungs would burst. Lactic acid burned through my thighs, and my cheeks felt on fire. But it did the job. The more I ran and the more I pushed myself, the more I felt the coiled-up tension in me begin to relax and unravel. My pack mates took lovers, but right now I dare not. I felt on the edge of insanity, the truth being that a deep need for vengeance burned through my soul. I could not risk hurting someone, mentally or physically, so I would keep my distance unless the need of release got too great and went beyond what my own hand could provide.

I'd told my stepmother feelings got you killed.

I'd meant fluffy, lovey-dovey shit.

Hatred would fuel me through to victory. Of that, I was sure.

Feeling much better, I took a steadier pace back to the compound, heading to the large wooden cabin I shared with the other six pack council members. Now drenched in sweat, I desperately needed a shower.

Walking inside, I found some of them writhing around the living room floor with one of the pack females. My 'brothers' liked to share.

I strolled past them as if they weren't naked and hard, either jerking off or balls deep in a hole. They just waved to me in greeting, because this was nothing unusual, and they knew better than to ask if I wanted to join in.

In all the years I'd known them I never had. Knowing that one day I'd be the alpha was another reason I'd kept that side of myself private and out of the compound.

Once the shower was running hot, I stepped underneath it and washed off the day. I felt I'd done enough that sleep would take me and then tomorrow we would stake out the woods. We had another delivery coming and if our enemy planned on dropping off another parcel, this time one of us would be waiting.

Chapter 4

Snow

"Are you sure you won't come with us to Windermere?" Mum asked me for what felt like the trillionth time, her eyebrows drawing together.

I shook my head. "Not this time. I'm going to make the most of having the castle to myself." My grin couldn't be contained.

"Can I stay with Snow?" Reid whined, pulling on Mum's arm.

Mum turned to him and folded her arms across her chest. "No, you most certainly cannot. You, son, need to see some fresh air and not an electronic screen," she chided.

He rolled his eyes at me when she wasn't looking.

"Iris is around should you need her. It will be very strange you not being with us," Mum said, moving away from Reid to give me a final hug and leaning in to kiss my cheek. She hung onto me a fraction longer than necessary.

"You're only going for four nights, not four years," I replied bemused. "Now be off with you all and leave me to enjoy some peace and solitude… especially from Reid."

My youngest brother stuck his tongue out at me.

"It's just leaving you when it's still your birthday. It doesn't seem right." Her expression looked pained.

"Yes, well that's when the house was available for rental, and it's not like you didn't celebrate with me already," I reassured her. They were off to stay in a place my mum found on her travels years ago and we'd revisited at least annually since. "Honestly, Mum, I'm looking forward to staying here alone, and Iris is only a shout away."

Mum nodded her head, finally resigned to the situation. "Hope work goes okay. Right, gang, let's get on our way," Mum said, finally allowing me some personal space, and they all began trooping out towards the minibus. Dad was the last to leave and say his goodbyes to me.

"I'm but a swoop away, Snow," my father said pulling me into his arms and giving me a squeeze.

"I know, Dad."

"Enjoy your days of freedom, darling. I know your mother is a little suffocating at times." He smirked.

"She's a wonderful mum, but I'm not denying my excitement at having a few days to myself. Ours is a busy and bustling household."

"It is. Even though our home is large, it can still be difficult to find solitude at times within its walls. Your mother always enjoyed a stroll to the lake, but I know you're not one for walking. Perhaps now you have the bike you might travel a little more. The bike means you can go at a more leisurely pace and take in the sights, as opposed to how we usually just sprint or fly off anywhere that doesn't require luggage. Don't forget you can work anywhere in the world, sweetheart." I was currently a hotel receptionist, working from six pm to two am, five days a week.

"Are you trying to get rid of me?" I joked.

He smiled. "Not in the slightest, but there's a whole world out there waiting to be explored, and while your mother isn't watching might be a time to start. And it's not like you'll need to take annual leave because I'm guessing you already did. I know if I was in your position I would have done so," he added with a knowing gaze.

"Busted," I replied, and we both laughed.

He left to join the others. I watched the minibus leave the estate, waving until it had gone out of sight.

As it did, a tingle jumped around my tummy, and I ran around the hallway jumping and cheering. I had the whole castle to myself and while I was under no illusion that Iris would be checking up on me, I was going to make the most of things.

The first thing I did was run around the whole house, just as I'd done when I was a small child with my sisters, except this time there was no mum telling us to be careful and to stop before we broke an antique.

The run was exhilarating, and made me crave more, so I got changed into some jogging bottoms and a sweatshirt. Then slipping my feet into my trainers, I locked the door behind me and set off towards our woods. The small amount of snow from the early hours of the morning had gone and the trees cast their shadows in the darkness.

Our woodland was a decent acreage and ended at the nearest towns' borders, but I ran circles around the lake rather than running to the edge. Faster and faster I ran, narrowly missing trees on occasion. I liked the gamble. Would my fast feet and nimbleness win, or would I hit my head on a thick trunk and render myself temporarily unconscious. I didn't particularly care either way but felt triumphant when I finally came to a halt and hadn't hit a single tree.

I stopped by the lake my mother loved, but it did nothing for me. Yes, it was pretty, but I liked movement and there was little here. Having finished with my woodland dash, I zoomed back to the house and headed towards our living room.

The large, sumptuous sofa was of course empty, a rarity indeed, and I sprawled out on it, stretching my limbs. I sunk down into its embrace and thought about what my father had said about potentially leaving the house and visiting places further afield. I did now have my bike and a few days off...

Could I do it?

Did I want to leave the house I'd finally got all to myself?

But looking around, I knew that within a day, if not within hours, my excitement at being alone would wane, and I'd be tempted to go join my family in the Lake District. And although that would not be the worst thing in the world, neither would it be a step towards independence. My father had obviously anticipated this, hence his words about me travelling more.

But where would I go?

I'd never gone further than the local towns on my own. Otherwise, I'd always been with family.

Have an adventure. Get on the bike and just set off, see where you end up, flashed through my mind. Like an itch that needed scratching, I became restless, and an hour or so later, I had a small backpack packed with essentials, and I climbed onto my bike. I sent Iris a text.

Snow: Dad recommended I do a bit of travelling, so I'm just off out on the bike. I might stay over somewhere, or I might come back to the castle later. I'll keep you informed. DO NOT TELL MUM!!!!

Locking up the castle behind me, I added the keys and phone to my backpack and after climbing aboard my bike, I drove out of the estate, only stopping to ensure the security gates closed properly.

I cycled for hours. Once past the familiar towns, I drank in the vistas of the unfamiliar. The different sizes and architecture of the housing, the parks. I noted which had luscious green areas and which were concrete jungles. I stopped to admire the art of some graffiti and cycled past the travesty of other random scrawls across shop windows and road signs. There were gangs of youths who kicked walls and jeered at passers-by, lacking something else to do. One shouted, 'What the fuck are you looking at, bitch?' as I rode past. I saw other young ones playing football, their families watching and cheering them on. The more I rode, the more I felt I was lucky to have the family I had, and the luxury we enjoyed.

Stopping near a large park surrounded by trees, I decided this would be the last place I'd look around today. Then I would turn back and return to the castle, and sleep in my own bed. In the future I might explore the world a little more, but this evening had made me so appreciative of everything I had that I hungered for the familiar; to pour over every bit of our estate and rejoice in its beauty. To look upon it as if I was seeing it for the first time. But first, I'd fasten up my bike and have a stroll around this park, because it had an old-fashioned bandstand and water features and deserved my attention.

As I was completely relaxed, my focus fixed on the fountain, I did not expect to find a chain looped around my neck. I grabbed at it, using every bit of my strength to try to free myself. It couldn't kill me—I didn't breathe. But it had incapacitated me, and I was being dragged towards the wooded area. Trying to dig my heels in the earth resulted in two churned mud tracks side by side that resembled a youth having gone rogue on his dirt-bike.

The further I was pulled into the woods, the more I smelled wolves. Oh fuck, this was not where I needed to be. I had to get away from my mystery assailant. Now on the floor, on my back, I was being pulled along a dirt path, stones hard under my body. Thank goodness for the protective leathers I'd found on my bed as an extra birthday present. A note from my mum had said she'd feel better if I wore them. My helmet protected my hair from being torn off on route to wherever the hell we were headed. I tried to grab onto anything I could to gain some leverage, but all that happened were branches broke off in my hands. Terror flooded my body. There was a vast difference between the safety of agreed physical contact versus an unknown attacker.

I couldn't scent my attacker, could smell nothing but the wolf territory. I had to get back on my feet. The need to better my enemy fuelled me, the fact I may get hurt not bothering me in the slightest if it meant my escape. So instead of trying to stop myself, I completely relaxed.

The moment I did so, I flew backwards like lightning as the force of the drag against my former resistance now meant I was like an elastic band. My assailant was taken off their feet as I hit them like a bowling ball.

Strike!

I was up on my feet, but so were they, and before I could work out my next move, the 'shadow', which was what I quickly named the person encased entirely in black with shades over their eyes, punched me so hard in the face that I hit a tree behind me. I had no chance as they advanced on me quickly. My helmet was removed, and more punches rained down hard on my head until the world faded out.

My eyes opened, and pain enveloped me like the worst migraine. Turning to the side, I threw up, red blood coating the woodland floor like spilled wine. It ran under a black wooden box, and I stretched out and pulled the box towards me, wondering what it was and why it had been placed there.

At the same time, my senses returned with a vengeance, and I smelled wolf so strongly it was like they were right beside me...

With dread and the slowest pace I'd ever moved at, I turned my body to face the front, not wanting to do anything that meant the wolf/wolves saw me as a threat.

And there two of them were. Although panic set through my body like a brain freeze, that wasn't all that happened. Because these two men had to be the most attractive men I'd ever seen. Oh, I'd heard that wolf shifters were beautiful creatures when in their furry forms, but I hadn't known that carried through to their human selves too.

One man had white hair, pale skin, and the lightest blue eyes I'd ever seen, and the other was like his negative: dark hair, dark skin, brown eyes that were like looking into two pools of a black hole. Both were disconcerting: for their striking features and also for the hate that lingered in both their gazes.

This was not good.

"So what's in the box this time?" the dark haired one enquired. "I have to say, and no insult intended, but we did not think our enemy was a girl. Or are you just a messenger?"

"What the fuck are you talking about?" I snapped, unable to stop myself, but my head was throbbing. My wounds would have cleared but the lingering trauma had not. "I've been attacked and left in these woods. I need to get home."

The sound of branches snapping and breaking and

footsteps heading nearer hurt my sensitive ears, everything amplified by the fact my head had been pounded like chicken breasts under a rolling pin. I placed my hands over my ears and scrunched up my eyes until it stopped.

Opening them, I startled at being towered over by the largest man I'd ever seen. He was so broad I felt his muscles must be as large as boulders, but as my gaze finished tracking his body and finally met his eyes, I realised that the hate in the other wolves' gazes had nothing on the disgust and vitriol levelled at me now.

"You have trespassed on our land, though that is the least of your problems. You are now our prisoner, and we will find out everything about why you have that box," the guy growled out. He had golden blonde hair with streaks of russet and eyes that looked like fire. I should have been petrified, but for some reason unknown to me, I was not.

He turned to the other wolves. "Bring her to the cabin," he said.

Chapter 5

Kellan

I'd been ready to turn in for the evening when my phone rang.

"Kellan, a couple of the cameras have stopped working."

Adrenaline shot through my system. While Diego told me he and Trent were off to the woods to see what was happening, I ran up the stairs.

"Pierce!" I yelled in the direction of his bedroom. Reaching the room next to mine, I threw open his bedroom door, to find he had his headphones on while playing a game. He startled, his eyes widening, and quickly removed them.

"The cameras stopped working. Diego and Trent are going to see if there's anything happening in the woods. Can you go see what the fuck is wrong with the cameras."

"Fuck. Yes. On it. Sorry, Raina, we'll have to catch this up another time," he said, following me back downstairs and out of the door.

Raina. That woman spread herself like mould. She loved playing games all right and I'd bet there was motive behind playing them live with Pierce. But he was a grown man and while she was bothering him, she wasn't bothering me.

My phone rang again as I got to the edge of the woods. I saw spots in my vision and my fingers tingled. *Get a grip, Kellan.*

"Yes?" I uttered.

"We've found a female unconscious laid beside another black box. She's a vampire." Diego gave me their location.

"Do *not* give her any opportunity to escape," I yelled, and I began running to the place he'd described, slowing down as I got nearer, so I could appear cool, calm, and collected in front of my friends and the woman, though I was anything but. My hands were tight fists, and if I found out this woman was responsible for my father's death, I knew I'd change and destroy her. But I needed to make sure she was guilty first.

My mouth dropped open as I witnessed this slip of a young woman, currently sat with her knees up, eyes scrunched closed, and with her hands on her ears. She wore protective leathers and trainers, and her long dark hair was dishevelled. It appeared our actual enemy had sent their next 'gift' with a sacrificial lamb. No way was she the main character in this ongoing vendetta. I stood staring at her, waiting for her plea of innocence. My two fellow wolves kept silent throughout, anticipating my next order.

After finally opening her eyes, rather than quivering in fear, the woman looked me up and down as if I was a tasty rib. That's when I realised I'd made my first mistake; underestimating a female vampire. Wily and deceitful as a species, of course she could be our enemy.

"You have trespassed on our land, though that is the least of your problems. You are now our prisoner, and we will find out everything about why you have that box," I snarled at her. All she did was continue to stare, but this time directly in my eyes. I broke eye contact to turn to Trent and Diego. "Bring her to the cabin."

"I don't know anything about the box, and I need your help," she said. Her voice indicated wealth and piqued my interest.

Diego headed for the box and Trent for the

woman. She scuttled backwards away from him. "I-I've been attacked and lost my belongings. Can you at least see if you can find any of my things? I had a backpack with my phone and keys in it and some clothes and toiletries, and I locked my electric bike against a tree. They dragged me in here—"

I interrupted. "—a vampire with an electric bike?" I scoffed. "What bullshit."

Her gaze darted around her, and I readied myself for a potential escape attempt, but instead she gripped the ends of her coat sleeves. "You need to listen to me. I was exploring. I don't get to take in the sights when I'm speeding around. Whoever you're looking for dragged me here and beat me unconscious."

Trent turned to me for an answer, but I raised a hand. "Could be a trap. We take her to the cabin first and then we'll search around for any belongings."

"It's not a trap," the woman pleaded, her words rushing out. "I was attacked. I need you to contact my family." She sounded convincing, but then a good liar would.

"You're coming to our cabin where you can explain yourself further and then we'll take it from there," I said with forced restraint. What I wanted to do was place my hands around her neck and make her spill her story, but the fact she could be innocent in all this stopped me from doing so—for now.

"I'm going to help you to your feet and then put you over my shoulder to transport you to the cabin," Trent told her. "No sudden moves, or *he'll* deal with you, and it won't be with the manners I'm affording you," he explained.

The woman nodded her assent.

"What's your name?" he asked her.

"Snow," she answered. "My name is Snow. What's yours?"

I saw the amusement skitter across Trent's features. "I'm Trent. The blonde one is Diego, and the alpha will let you know who he is when he feels like it," he said. Her gaze snapped to mine.

That dark brown hair and those doe-like brown eyes made me think of an orphaned deer, like bloody Bambi. Even more so as she was helped to her feet and staggered slightly. I felt my cock twitch and honestly could have punched myself in the dick in disgust. The sooner we questioned her the better.

"I'll see you at the cabin," I said, and I took off back through the woods.

I reached the cabin ahead of the other two, and on entering found Ace and Samuel sitting on one of the three sofas, alongside Nala.

"Well?" Nala demanded, with the air of a former alpha's mate. She realised immediately that she no longer was able to carry such airs and graces and she swallowed visibly before looking at the floor.

I answered her anyway. Nala would get used to the new regime in time. First, she wanted to avenge the death of her husband, and with that came a fierce determination, the emphasis on *fierce*.

"We've captured a female vampire on the periphery of our compound. She hasn't said much beyond that she was attacked and asked us to search for her belongings. Trent is on his way back with her and Diego will be bringing back the box we found by her side."

"A *box* box?" Ace asked.

"Yes. The same that we've received in the past, which is why we're bringing the woman here for questioning." The door began to open as I finished speaking.

"Where to?" Trent asked.

"Time out," I said. "You sit outside the cell while we discuss things out here."

"Okay, Boss," he answered, and headed around the back where we had a padded room with two 'cells'.

Sometimes wolves got hot-headed and needed a 'time out', and the room had been put together accordingly.

"Just to say that I'll need to feed in the morning," Snow announced, all matter of fact and no longer sounding nervous. All the seated wolves' heads snapped towards her. "If I don't, I'll get mega vampire cranky. Just giving you a heads-up so you can get me some, or maybe catch me a small animal. Obviously letting me go would be best, but if I'm not free to leave by then, I honestly will need to feed. Otherwise, I'll be impossible to deal with, before eventually becoming weak and unresponsive," she added.

I cursed under my breath.

"Don't say I didn't warn you." She shrugged, still upside down and laid over Trent's back.

"Time out," I repeated with force, and Trent marched off towards the back room.

"Anyone else mightily surprised by the new prisoner?" Samuel asked, looking at the others.

"Not exactly petrified, was she? Makes me think she is involved with Santos' murder," Nala said.

"The fact she's telling us what she needs, does not make her a criminal," Samuel argued. "It just means she's looking out for herself."

"She was nervous, but we've reassured her on the way here that if she's innocent she will come to no harm," Diego noted. "Let's proceed with caution, but innocent until proven guilty, remember?"

Nala nodded.

My phone rang. Pierce.

"What have you found?"

"Whoever it is found a way for the cameras to be disrupted. I'm thinking they had some kind of signal blocker. By the time I came here all the cameras were working again. I saw you've captured a female. Is she the murderer?"

"I don't know. We're still questioning her. She maintains she was attacked, but without CCTV we can't know."

"Even if it's not her, the fact remains that this time they managed to get onto our actual property. They're stepping up their game, Kellan."

I sighed. "I know."

"What's in the box?" Pierce asked.

"I don't know. We've not opened it yet. Hold on," I said, and I turned to Diego.

"Open it."

Diego placed the box on the coffee table and removed the red ribbon. Removing the lid from the box he peered inside.

"It's a tongue," he stated.

When my father's head had been sent previously, his tongue had been removed.

"Is the note the same as usual?" I checked.

Diego lifted the note and I watched his eyes skim the words. He shook his head. "No, it's different."

"Read it aloud," I ordered.

Diego cleared his throat.

A tongue returned
   But unable to form words
   Mine still present
   But never observed
   My life ruined piece by piece
   I'll do unto others
   As they have done to me.

"More riddles," I noted. "Diego, take Ace out with you and go search for this backpack, bike, and anything else that may be on the outskirts of our property. Everyone else, you're excused. I'm going to see what I can get out of our new prisoner."

"What about the blood she asked for?" Nala reminded me.

"Godammit. Can you sort that?" I asked her. She nodded.

"Thanks," I said. I turned my attention back to the phone. "Did you hear all that, Pierce?"

"Yes, Boss."

"I need you to look into additional security. Whatever we need you let me know."

"Already on it," he confirmed.

"Thank you. I'll catch up with you later," I said. Then I stood and let out a large exhalation, before striding towards the time out room.

Our astute prisoner had Trent smiling at her.

I would kick his arse seven ways to Sunday when we were outside this room for being a sucker for a pretty face. Actually, no she was the sucker... a bloodsucker. We were all immune to the compulsion that vampires used, otherwise shifters would have been become extinct centuries ago, but we weren't immune to attraction.

Snow kept her eyes on me through the bars of one of the cells as I asked Trent to leave us alone. Once he'd departed, I took his vacated seat positioned in front of the cell. She held her chin high as she waited for me to speak.

"Tell me how you came to be where we found you. Every bit of it," I ordered.

"But I just told Trent," she protested.

I lifted my palms up in a 'who cares' gesture. "Good. I'll be able to check with him that your story matches." I paused for emphasis. "Only, liars have a habit of tripping over their bullshit."

"I'm not a liar." She was still staring at me with those beguiling eyes, her lips now pinched together.

I sat back in the seat, slumping a little with my legs stretched out in front of me like I had all the time in the world. "Please begin," I said, ignoring her.

"It's my birthday today," she began. My eyes widened in surprise. That wasn't what I'd expected her to start with. "My parents bought me an electric bike as a gift, and I went out on it later this afternoon. During the evening, I made my way to the park, and I'd decided on one last walk around before returning home." Those nostrils flared again. "I was attacked. A chain was placed around my neck, and they dragged me through the woods. I have no idea who attacked me as they were entirely covered in black, and I could discern no recognisable scent from them because of the overpowering scent of wolves everywhere, especially wolf piss. They hit me repeatedly in the head until I passed out. That's all I remember until I woke up with a thumping headache, nausea, and saw Trent and Diego. I can't have been unconscious long though because, well, vampire. I heal quick."

"And who gave you the box?"

"No one gave me the box. It was at the side of me when I came to. I know my attacker didn't carry a box though. Either they placed it there afterwards or someone else did."

"What did this attacker look like?"

"Taller than me, by a head. Wider than me. But they were disguised, and I barely saw them seeing as they dragged me and then beat me." She rubbed at her eye. "I thought this person mean to hurt me, like they'd hung around the park looking for a lone female. But now I'm guessing I was just in the wrong place at the wrong time. You clearly have some dispute going on with someone. I'm going to plump for the fact they thought I was one of you. A wolf."

"You're nothing like a wolf," I uttered with disdain.

"I'm dressed like you are," she noted, casting her eyes down over my leather pants and then to my jacket.

"Fuck." She was right. Her leather trousers and

jacket did look like something a female wolf would wear if she was out.

"I need my stuff," she said. "My mother always told me to memorise phone numbers, but I thought I knew better. Now I don't have a phone and can't call her because I don't remember anyone's number."

"You can't call her anyway because you're my prisoner," I reminded her.

"Prisoners get a phone call, don't they?" she pushed.

"Not this time."

She interlinked her fingers and placed them atop her head. "Can you *please* send someone to search for my belongings? Then when you have my phone, I can call my parents, and get the hell out of here. No disrespect, but I prefer my own place."

I sat forward. "I've sent two wolves out looking for your things. No disrespect, but if you're innocent I'll not get rid of you fast enough. Your kind isn't welcome here."

"My *kind*?"

She looked about to tear a strip off me for being anti-vampire, but then her posture relaxed, and she sat back on her seat, hands on her lap. It appeared we'd swapped roles, because now she looked like she had the upper hand.

"Ah, a vampire did something to you." Leaning forward, she peered into my eyes. "Yeah, they did something very, very bad." She sat back again, her finger tapping on her lips. "The box," she said, her eyes widening. "It's tied to that, isn't it? What's in the box?"

"I'm the one asking the questions," I snarled. I was on the attack because this woman was getting under my skin, and I didn't like that one little bit.

Chapter 6

Snow

A whole world out there waiting to be explored and within one evening I'd managed to get myself trapped in a wolf's lair. And while to begin with I'd felt petrified, now my natural instincts had kicked in, my survival ones. This had calmed me somewhat. I knew one thing for sure. When my father found out, this arrogant arsehole would be torn a new one.

The thought made me smile.

"Something amusing about being a captive, is there?" The alpha's eyebrows furrowed and then released.

"I'm just thinking about how my father will tear you apart piece by piece when he finds out what you've done with his precious daughter."

He flinched. Something I'd said had hit home

hard. Clearly, someone near to him had been badly harmed or killed by a vampire. That's why he looked upon me with such hatred. That's why I was imprisoned. Looking at him now, at the tight set of his jaw, my pleas of innocence were going to get me nowhere. I'd have to tread carefully while I hoped and prayed the others found my belongings.

"My mother spent years imprisoned in a basement," I informed him, changing the subject.

"Was she as chatty as you?" he retorted. "If so, I see the appeal."

"Are you always this charming?" I asked, not rising to his baiting.

The alpha stared at me as if I was a puzzle he couldn't find a single clue for. Any minute now he was going to punch a wall if his tightened fists were any indication.

"Why aren't you frightened?" he asked eventually.

"I am frightened," I answered truthfully. "I'm being held captive in a strange place by wolves and accused of some mysterious wrongdoing when I'm innocent. But I'm not going to sit in front of you shaking and begging you to release me. Not yet anyway. Right now, I'm hoping the wolves return with my belongings, you realise I was telling the truth, and then you let me go. That way I can get back home before my godmother realises I didn't return from my bike ride and raises the alarm. If that happens, you'll be the one begging to be let go when my father gets hold of you."

"I'm not scared of a vampire," he drawled out.

I huffed. "It's more the fact he's my father you need to worry about than the fact he's a vampire. He's very protective of his children after waiting a long time to become a dad. Are you a father?"

"No."

"Are you going to tell me your name?" I pushed. "You know mine. I don't think it's very polite that you haven't introduced yourself. Were you not raised properly?"

Those knuckles of his were white such was his clenching of them now. I was getting under his skin and to be honest was finding it quite amusing. If you'd have asked me how I would behave if captured and imprisoned by an alpha wolf this wouldn't have been it at all. The fact he was so damn attractive, even more so when rattled, was clearly making my vampire teasing ramp up. This man held me as a prisoner, but I was treating him as my prey.

"You have no need of knowing my name," he gritted out as the door opened and one of the wolves entered. This one a redhead.

"Hey, Kellan. We found a bike, an abandoned helmet, and this." The man raised his hand which carried my backpack. "Looks like she was telling the truth."

"Pass me the bag and then leave," Kellan ordered, flexing his fingers in a 'come forward' instruction.

The man did as asked.

"Can I go now, *Kellan*?" I asked, giving him a smug smile.

He ignored me as he unfastened the bag and began lifting out items. From the front pocket he retrieved my phone and keys. Then he went into the back and brought out two dresses, my pyjamas, and then my lacy underwear. My pink thong looked so tiny in his giant hands. His face was a mask of stillness as he continued going through my belongings, until he brought out the red ribbon I liked to tie in my hair. He lifted and stared at it like it dripped blood. His skin mottled with rage.

What the hell had been triggered by that of all things?

"You try to protest your innocence and yet you carry such a huge clue in your backpack of being very involved in our current situation. You will remain our prisoner until you admit your part in the attack on one of our own." He placed the ribbon in his pocket, and stuffed everything else back in the backpack, throwing that on the ground and leaving him with only my phone.

"Tell me who I need to text to assure them you're safe and well."

"But I'm not."

"Don't play games with me, little Bambi. I'm granting you a kindness right now of time. I could always stake you through your heart and find out where to send the dust."

Bambi?

I sighed. Right now, I had more of concern than a stupid nickname.

"My phone code is 5103. Once unlocked, please go into WhatsApp and send a message to Iris that I've found a B&B in Pladstone and I'm staying another night." Pladstone had been one of the places I'd passed through that had been green and pretty.

"Good, your location services are turned off already," Kellan noted.

"That's because my kind can scent each other. I hadn't needed those services until you kidnapped me."

He typed and sent the message.

A few minutes later a reply came.

"Iris says to have fun and to keep her informed of your whereabouts, but to also be careful. Oops, too late."

I ignored him.

"Why didn't you have me text your mother or father?" he asked.

I stayed silent.

"They're not home, are they?" he guessed, but I didn't respond either way. Instead, I changed the subject.

"That box had a red ribbon on it. I remember now. So because I wear one in my hair, you think I have something to do with it. Well, I don't. It's just my signature style." I pushed on. "If you tell me what's been happening, maybe I can help you? I probably can't, but I might have some ideas on your next moves."

"My next move is to leave you in here to think about whether you're going to admit to your involvement in the delivery of that box."

I sighed with frustration. "I didn't deliver it. You found it next to me. It was left there after my attack. How many more times?"

"But you have no signs of being attacked, do you?"

"Of course not. I'm a vampire. I healed. But the shadow person clearly was satisfied that they'd beaten me up long enough for me to stay unconscious until you found me. Don't you have CCTV to prove my innocence?"

He didn't answer for a while.

"I have much to consider," he finally said. "And while I do, you will stay here in this room," he announced, and then he left me on my own.

I stared at the closed door for a while, wondering if Kellan would return, or if he'd send another wolf to watch over me. I fully expected a 'good cop' wolf after the bad one had exited. It didn't really matter given I'd done nothing wrong.

The truth was, I still had questions of my own. Had I been followed? Who had placed the box by my head? And what was happening with these wolves? I needed to find out as soon as possible.

Gripping hold of the bars, I tried to pull them apart to see if I could escape the cell. But of course, if they held in wolves they also held in my own kind. Damn. I could feel fury rising inside me. I was innocent, and they were wasting the time I was supposed to have to myself.

You have got time to yourself. Just in a cell, my quirky brain thought. *Very funny*, I noted. Soon I was bored rigid, but my body poised to attack, the no doubt natural state of a captive vampire, I guessed. I shouted and yelled and screamed for someone to come get me, but all my pleas were left unanswered.

The urge came upon me once more to find solace within pain, and I threw myself at the bars. Over and over and over. When that didn't work, I tried the wall behind me.

"What in the holy fuck is going on in here?" Kellan yelled at the top of his lungs as he burst into the room.

I stood there, knowing my eyes would be red, my fangs descended. I could feel blood running down my cheeks and my fists. Both would heal, but slowly, given I needed to feed now. I'd soon need to sleep too. Dawn was breaking, and while my kind could be out in daylight and didn't fry in the light, we naturally were nocturnal in habit.

I must have looked to Kellan like a madwoman. I possibly was.

"You can't escape. You must know that?" he finally voiced.

"Of course I know that," I replied.

"Then why are you throwing yourself at the bars as if you might break through them? Even if you succeeded, there's another locked door, and then wolves outside. You're wasting your time." he snapped.

"On the contrary. I'm keeping myself occupied

while I'm just stuck here like a rat in a trap," I told him.

"Wouldn't it be better to do some regular exercise? There's room to do squats."

I smashed myself into the front bars of the cell again. I felt my upper lip split, and blood poured, dripping into my mouth. I licked it. My saliva would help seal the wound. Gripping the bars, I stared through them at Kellan, my eyes boring into his. I felt wild. "This *is* my exercise. Do you know when my mother was human and my father took her in, she craved the captivity she'd left behind? For years she slept in a large birdcage. Once turned, she slowly rejected that which she'd known, because vampires like their space. We're swift, we're strong, we take up space. You run, wolf. Imagine someone bound your legs and yet that urge to dash through your woods burned within you. Would you be satisfied with a push-up? Of course not. You need the burn in your thighs, the wind whipping your hair. Perhaps the need to fuck or to feed. Now soon, I will fall asleep, and on waking I *will* need to feed." I tilted my head. "I have one final request, Alpha Kellan, before you leave me to slumber."

He raised a brow. "What makes you think I'll grant that request?"

"Because once actioned, I'll be quiet for a time.

Otherwise, you can continue to hear me scream and throw myself around this small space again and again until I tire completely."

He sighed. "What's your request?"

"Let me out of this cell for a short time." I saw his head twist to the left as he began his refusal. "Hear me out, please. Like you said, the door is a further barrier and then there's the living room. I need to use this padded room to exhaust myself."

A minute passed before resignation reigned on Kellan's face. "I'll be back in a moment after I've warned my fellow pack members to prepare for the possibility of a vampire flying out of the door." He left, but quickly returned, bringing the redhead with him.

"Ace will unlock the door to the cell. I will stand guard over here," he informed me. "Any funny business and I'll put you back in the cell and bind you, so you can't move an inch."

"Understood." I rose and waited for Ace to put the key in the lock. He gazed at me as if he were a mouse eying a piece of cheese, wondering if it was a treat or a trap. "I just want to stretch my limbs," I tried to reassure him, but he still gave me a wide berth as I walked out of the confines of the cell.

"Are you going to watch?" I asked Kellan, teasingly.

"We both are," he replied, his voice devoid of emotion.

"I like to watch," Ace quipped. "Only usually it's a little more enjoyable than this.

I turned to him, smirking. "Is that right?" I winked at him. At least one of these wolves had a personality.

"You've got two minutes starting from NOW," Kellan snapped.

I raced to his side of the room, reaching him in the blink of an eye. Deliberately invading his personal space, I stood with only a millimetre separating our bodies. His breath came sharp. "Thanks for this," I said before I sprinted to the side of the cell I'd been inside, passing Ace and throwing myself at the padded wall. Back and forth I went, thudding into wall after wall until I felt the fizz within my body finally give way and cease. Then I slumped to the floor.

"Would you put me back now please? I just hope you'll let me feed tomorrow," I managed to utter before my eyes closed.

I vaguely felt large warm hands lift me and carry me back into the cell.

Chapter 7

Kellan

By the time I crawled beneath my sheets at around four am, I was mentally and physically exhausted. Yet sleep wouldn't come. Every time I closed my eyes, I saw Snow. Replayed every part of our conversation in my head. I was trying to find clues in her words, trying to work out if she was innocent or as guilty as hell.

The woman was like none I'd ever met before. Maybe the first woman after my dear departed mother who freely challenged me. Here I was the alpha, and no woman would dare, not even Nala.

My encounters with female vampires were few and at a distance, due to the odd meetings between shifter and vampire councils, but did they all behave like

Snow; hurting themselves in order to disperse energy? I had no clue. Rolling over onto my side, I grabbed my phone from my bedside table and sat up, typing into the search bar: *the traits of female vampires.*

According to the internet there wasn't any discernment between them and their male counterparts: pale, heightened senses, didn't ever seem to age beyond around thirty physically unless turned from an older human. Male vampires became fertile for five years every fifty years, meaning that the female could have a long time to wait before motherhood. Both could be seductive, especially if they used compulsion, also known as 'the thrall'. That wouldn't work on me. But the fact Snow was excruciatingly beautiful had my thoughts in knots that I didn't wish to unravel. But being attracted to her pretty face didn't negate the fact that I hated her kind.

Getting out of bed completely, I visited my bathroom to empty my bladder, and then on the way back I reached for the bottle of scotch I had on the top of my chest of drawers. I took the bottle to bed and drank slowly but steadily until the booze mellowed me enough that I passed out.

I woke to find myself next to a soaking puddle of whisky from where the bottle had fallen out of my hand. At least it had done the trick in getting me to sleep. Picking up the bottle, which still had around a sixth of its contents left, I headed to the bathroom, dropping the scotch back on the chest of drawers on the way.

Though I ached to go see what was happening with our prisoner, I was doing nothing until I'd had a shower and washed the previous day off myself.

Finally feeling more alive and awake, I ventured downstairs for an update. We'd set a rota on checking on our 'guest' and Samuel was on the sofa watching TV as I walked into the living space.

"She's still asleep, Boss. Nothing to report. She's not woken at all."

"Thanks. I'm going to call a meeting. We need to make a plan of action because we have a vampire in a cell, but we're still no further forward in finding out what happened to my father."

"Okay."

"You can go. I'll handle things for now until it's time for Pierce to take over."

Samuel didn't need telling twice. He'd left the room within thirty seconds. I went to the time out room because I wanted to make sure our prisoner was asleep and not dead. How long could they survive without feeding? I had no idea.

Unlocking the door and pushing it open, I walked into the room and over to the other side, my eyes falling on Snow. I'd not thought to let her get changed, so she still wore the leather jacket, t-shirt, and leather trousers she'd turned up in. Laid on her side with one leg curled up and one straight, the leather pants hugged her butt, and I couldn't help but let my eyes linger over her form. Then I remembered I was here to check she was sleeping. It was rare a vampire died from not feeding. Usually, they just became a shrivelled husk, but transfusion could bring them back. No, death was usually due to a stake to the heart or decapitation.

Sitting by her side, I rolled her over onto her back.

Nothing.

Because they didn't breathe, she just looked like a dead woman.

That's because she is, you dickhead.

Realising I was handling an evil vampire like a precious jewel, I changed tack and shoved at her arm roughly, before lifting her onto her feet and shaking her.

Snow stirred in my arms, opening her eyes. "Whasappening?" She was so tired she couldn't form words, but at least I knew I'd not let a potentially innocent woman die. When I left, I'd chase up Nala to ensure she got hold of the blood.

Snow's face was scrunched up in confusion, her eyes closing. She kept trying to open them but was struggling. I placed her back down to the floor, my mission done. So why did I not then leave the room? Why did I stay in the cell sitting alongside Snow on the padded floor? Maybe I was hoping for a clue or an answer. Because if she was innocent then I'd really fucked up. More disconcertingly though, I wondered why I even cared. Since my father's death, my heart had been encased in stone, my entire being uncaring, unfeeling. It was like I was made of ice. Now around this woman I was experiencing emotions: hatred, dislike, lust, guilt. No one else had got through to me, yet this potential enemy was getting a reaction.

Why?

Snow's eyes opened slightly again, and she whispered. I leaned in closer trying to discern what she was mumbling.

"Fuck off, or I'll sample you for breakfast. I'm starving," she muttered.

I couldn't help it. I smirked. The woman was amusing. I'd give her that.

"I'm organising food. I'll be back," I said. But her eyes had closed again, and she was out for the count.

By eleven am, everyone but Pierce was assembled in the boardroom. Pierce was present via videocall while sitting on the sofa close to the time out room. Nala was in the room, although no longer the alpha's mate. She would be offered a position of advisor to the council at my official naming ceremony as she carried a wealth of knowledge. However, I'd postponed the event until we'd solved my father's murder.

"Okay, everyone. I'll try to make this fast. I gather by the silence there's been nothing to report. No additional boxes delivered, no more cameras stopping, or anything else that would warrant attention?"

They all said no.

"I'm aware this situation is frustrating, but we will find the enemy," I paused, "if we haven't already."

"What's the latest with Snow?" Ace asked.

I blew out a frustrated breath. I might be the alpha, but I was honest if I didn't have the answers.

"She still maintains her innocence. However," I pulled the red ribbon from my pocket, placing it on the table, "the fact I found this in her backpack still makes me think she could be involved. I have her phone," I said, wanting to smack myself in the face for the fact I'd placed in back in the backpack and forgotten about it, distracted by the woman herself. "I'll go through it in depth and see if there are any clues as to her involvement. If not, then I have to consider letting her go, and keeping watch on her from a distance."

Nala's lips crimped together, but I didn't challenge her. If she wanted to add something she would.

"Diego and Tommo, I want you to comb the woods again, inch by inch to see if you can find anything that might help us. Samuel and Ace, I want you to do the same with the park, concentrating on the area where we found Snow's belongings. Because either she is involved, or she was attacked like she insists. Either way, let's try to find something to help us progress. Nala, if you'd take over from Pierce around four pm, and be ready with the blood that Snow will require."

Nala nodded. "I've a delivery coming around one."

I nodded back in return.

"Pierce, I know you're dealing with the cameras, but later could you look over the physical evidence again? I'm sure it's a waste of time, but you've the keenest eye of us all."

"Of course," he said.

"Any other business?" I asked.

Everyone shook their heads and so I dismissed them, asking Ace to call back to the house and bring me Snow's backpack.

When they'd gone, I got up myself and walked through to the main office that adjoined the meeting room. My father's presence hit me immediately and I had to stand tall and breathe deeply in order to push the emotion back down. He was still everywhere in this room. From the photo of the two of us on his bookcase, which might be face down now but was still present, to the chair he'd chosen, and his best pens scattered around the desk. I even felt like I could still smell his aftershave. I grabbed a fistful of my hair and pulled, needing the slight pain to distract me from what I wanted to do: to slump over and let it all in. But I couldn't. I was the alpha and I needed to hold it together to ensure the safety of us all.

After taking several deep breaths, I fired up the laptop and took care of a few items of business while I waited for the backpack to be delivered.

"Here you go," Ace said, after knocking on the office door and waiting to be called in.

"Thanks." I took the bag off him.

"Right, we're all off to comb the area," he informed me.

"Let me know if you find anything."

"Will do, Boss." He left, and I went through the backpack again. This time I went more carefully, shaking out the nightwear and spare clothing to ensure nothing was tucked within the fabric. At the sight of the lacy thongs, I immediately imagined them encased around that peachy arse. Of all the women to turn me on, the last person I needed to find myself attracted to was our potential mortal enemy. I needed to get laid if the sight of a thong was distracting me. I found a journal that said, 'My Private Confessions,' on the front. But the key to the lock dangled from it on a loop of cotton and the pages remained empty of writing.

Placing the items back in the bag apart from the phone, I went out to the kitchen to get myself a fresh hot drink before turning my attention to the device.

Nala still had a smaller office here. She'd assisted my father where she could. She'd not been in there much of late, but as I passed the door on the way down to the kitchen, I heard her voice.

> "I seek your advice, oh crystal ball.
> Am I still the female in charge of all?"

I rolled my eyes from outside the door. Nala believed in fortune telling and had of all things, a ball that conjured up images and spoke to her. To me it was nothing more than an electronic toy designed to fleece susceptible women of their money, and cheap they were not. But as long as it didn't interfere with my plans, she could have at it.

The electronic voice spoke back.

> "For now, you are the female lead.
> But I must advise that you take heed.
> Another is here and will accept her fate.
> That she will be the new alpha's mate
> But danger comes where this maiden goes,
> You shall need to make sure you're on your toes."

"Thank you, wise one," I heard Nala reply. I quickly moved away from the door. Hopefully, even though it was a pile of crap, those words would make Nala more receptive to taking a back seat with pack business, if she felt my mate would make herself known soon.

I plugged Snow's phone in to one of the spare chargers we kept around the place and put in the code to open the screen.

There was a notification of a WhatsApp message from this Iris woman, and a text from Snow's mother. I didn't look at either as I didn't want them giving a 'read' notification. I would wait until I was back with Snow herself so we could deal with answering them.

Instead, I went into the messages from other people that had already been opened. There was nothing of any interest until I came across a contact named 'Gym'.

Snow: Can you meet me at four?
Gym: For the usual?

Snow: Yes, I need it.
Gym: I'll be there.

These messages had been from the day before we'd captured her. And while it could be a simple message to a personal trainer, I had a gut feeling there was a lot more to it. It was a lead, even a weak one, and I'd take it.

I worked a little longer and then at ten to four I decided I'd take the blood from Nala if she was still around, and I'd cover the next shift myself and quiz Snow on the messages. But Nala's office door was locked.

It was still time to head home. I was itching to get into the time out room. So much so that I went from a brisk walk to a jog and then to an actual run, only slowing when I got within view as I didn't want to panic any of my roommates if they were home.

As I unlocked the door, no one seemed to be around, so I guessed Pierce had left to do his assigned work and Nala was in the room with Snow. Hopefully, Nala would have given Snow the blood and I could simply ask my questions.

I pushed open the door to the time out room and my heart stopped beating for a moment. Nala stood over Snow's weakened form with a stake in her hand. Snow tried to place a hand over herself, but it was no use. In front of my eyes Nala plunged the stake into Snow's chest, before realising I was in the room watching.

My wolf shuddered through me, and I leapt for the still open cage.

Chapter 8

SNOW

I'd woken up hungry and wondered if my captors would provide the blood I required or would deny me to try to extort information from me. I hoped they'd soon realise I had nothing to do with their ongoing drama.

I didn't need to use a toilet as vampires had no need, but *I sure could do with brushing my teeth,* I thought, feeling around them with my tongue. You had to have top-tip dental care when your teeth needed to last for centuries. A shower wouldn't go amiss either. However, I doubted an opportunity to clean myself would be offered to me at this point in time.

I stared around the cell and the rest of the room. I might ask for a book to read because I was bored with my own thoughts already today. Thinking of books reminded me of my sister and my birthday gifts and made me feel teary, but then I flinched, distracted, as a cramping pain contorted my guts and placed a hand on my belly.

A wolf entered the room.

"Hey there, I'm Pierce. Just checking in on you," he said, coming closer to the cage. "You okay?"

"Just hungry," I told him. "Any news on getting me some blood?"

"I know Nala is organising it and she's coming to take over from me in half an hour, so I should expect she'll bring it with her. How long can you go without?" he asked. Then he looked down at the floor as if he'd realised he might be getting too personal.

"I can manage about a week before I'd get too weak to move my limbs, but I wouldn't die," I answered, causing him to look back at me with interest. "I'd just become a shrivelled husk. But I'm experiencing painful pangs in my tummy, just like anyone extremely hungry would, and that will get worse. Plus, as time goes on, I'll start to thirst and then I become unpredictable as my body will override my brain in order to survive."

"That's fascinating," Pierce replied, and I could see he meant it. "Shall I sit for a while to keep you company, or would you rather be alone?"

"Please sit. I'm so bored," I pleaded.

He smiled. It was a lovely smile. I studied him. His face was lightly tanned, his eyes green, and his hair a dark blonde. He took the seat in front of my cell.

"Does your wolf resemble your colouring as a human?" I asked.

"My fur is the colour of my hair, a dark blonde, but all our eyes turn the yellow of wolves," Pierce explained. "Do vampires talk much of wolves?"

"I can only speak for myself, and my family, and we are quite isolated. My father is very protective. It's only been since my twentieth birthday that he actually suggested I begin to explore the world a little."

"And on your first night of freedom we captured you, right?" He grimaced.

I nodded in response. "Exactly. So if you do free me, I can probably expect to be stuck back within the confines of Moonstone for the considerable future," I said with sarcasm. "I'm not sure which would be worse, there or here if I'm honest."

"Oh dear." Pierce chuckled.

"My father will be bad, but my mother worse," I added.

"I have an overbearing mother," Pierce replied. "But not in wanting to keep me home and safe. She just asks me every five minutes when I'm going to settle down and provide cubs as the pack needs to keep bearing healthy future pack members."

"I'm guessing that's your worst nightmare?" I probed. This was my first glimpse into the life of any of this pack and I was truly intrigued.

He sucked his top lip in for a moment or two before finally saying, "It's complicated because wolves don't date like they used to date."

"Does anyone?" I countered. "It used to be you got a boyfriend until you didn't, but now you can see as many people as you like until you deem yourselves exclusive. It's like having to audition to be considered."

"Yup, I hear you. We're moving away from the stereotypes of old for sure. Are you dating anyone or seeing people out there in the world where you're not our prisoner?"

"Nope," I replied, popping the p.

"That was quite an emphatic reply. Are you not interested in seeking a partner?"

I paused to consider my response. Pierce was easy to talk to and very attractive. If I wasn't a prisoner and had met him in a bar, I'd be flirting with him, wolf or not. Should I be up front with him or keep myself to myself? Taking a judgement call based on my intuition I decided to be open with him.

"I've not met anyone who offers what I want.

That's possibly because I don't *know* what I want. I'm supposed to date another vampire, or a human willing to turn. But so far, meh."

That made Pierce chuckle again. I liked the sound of it.

"My mum believes in one true love," I told him.

"You don't?"

I shook my head. "No. I think you can have several true loves."

"Interesting."

"Why so?" I challenged.

"I believe the same."

"You do?" My head tilted towards him with curiosity.

"Absolutely. My fellow wolves and I often seek our pleasure by sharing one woman. I believe it's possible we could all love that one woman."

I gasped and watched Pierce's eyebrows furrow.

"You think I'm wrong?" he asked, with a bitter smile.

"No. Sorry. You've caught me by surprise with your statement. But yes, I agree, it's possible you could all love one woman, just the same as I could love one man at once or a few. Because everything is possible, right? I could also love men, women, non-binary. Love is love, right?"

Pierce's green gaze seemed to light up and he leaned over.

"Right! There are religions where men take more than one wife. It's man himself that puts these limits in place."

"That's so true."

There was a sound from outside the door. Pierce looked at his watch. "I'd better get ready. I've some work to do. Sounds like Nala just arrived."

I smiled at him. "Thanks for coming to talk to me, Pierce. You've distracted me from being hungry and I've really enjoyed our conversation. I don't know much outside of where I live and within the vampire community. I'd love to speak more if you have the time. If I'm still here, that is."

He gave me a genuine smile in return. "I'd like that too. And if you are innocent and freed, then maybe we could meet up some time to talk more?"

I could tell this was a friendly invitation, rather than a 'come on' from Pierce's open posture and lack of intensity.

"If I can get out of my house, then absolutely," I joked, laughing.

Pierce laughed back, and then headed for the door, pausing before he left.

"For what it's worth, I don't feel you're involved in

the murder of Kellan's father. I hope I don't learn I'm wrong," he said, leaving the room.

Missing the gasp that escaped my mouth.

No wonder Kellan was so furious. So angry and detached. His father had been murdered. Had the shoe been on the other foot and I found someone who might be involved, I'd hold them captive too. And I doubt I'd have been so tolerant. I'd have probably pushed my prisoner to their limits.

My mind flooded with thoughts of my own father. I couldn't bear to think of a world without him in it and I counted my blessings that vampires were immortal. Werewolves were not. Though they had longevity and could live for hundreds of years, time in their human form made them more vulnerable to death. That was one thing I did know about them.

The door re-opened, and Nala appeared.

"Hey, Snow, I've brought your breakfast... dinner... whatever you want to call it." She patted her pocket.

I gave her a nervous smile. "Thank you so much. My abdomen is cramping with hunger more frequently now," I explained. I was surprised when instead of handing it through the bars, Nala went to unlock the cell. I blinked in confusion.

"I'm expecting you to get a rush of energy due to having gone so hungry," she clarified. "Ace told me how you'd raced around the cell before. Pierce is standing by outside in case I call out for help, but I think we'll be fine." She walked in and towards me. "How are you feeling other than the pains?"

"Just a little weak," I said.

"That's understandable."

What happened next all seemed to happen within a beat in time.

Nala produced a stake from her pocket instead of the expected blood packet. As my eyes looked upon it in horror and widened, the door opened and Kellan walked in, distracting us both for a second. I saw his body ripple and russet fur appear, him in a half wolf/half human state as Nala plunged the stake into my chest.

I closed my eyes waiting for the end. But it didn't happen. Nala had missed my heart. While I writhed in agony from it still being deep within my body, I noted Kellan was now pure wolf and Nala had also changed, her wolf one of black fur. They were both outside of the cell, circling each other. Even on my knees, feeling close to passing out through the agony, I could note how beautiful they both were.

As I retched—nothing coming up as I had nothing in my stomach—I knew I needed to pull out the stake. I just had to hope it wasn't next to my heart as I would need to wiggle it free. Clasping my hand around the edge, I placed my other on my chest at the side of the stake and I began to attempt to free my body of the unwanted addition.

"Orrrrrrh," I groaned as it moved within my tissues. The pain was overwhelming and nothing like what I subjected myself to with Andre. Seemed I did have limits to what I could endure and enjoy. Counting to three, one painful grimace per count, I pulled with every ounce of my last strength until I was free of the stake. I felt the puncture wound knit back together and I *did* enjoy every minute of *that* feeling.

Slumping in relief, I saw the blood packet in the doorway of the cell where it had fallen as Nala had changed to wolf form. The pain had all but depleted me of energy, but a fierce determination had me pull myself inch by inch across the floor, resting in between.

By this time, I'd lost interest in the wolf battle, my vision narrowed to the packet on the floor. Within reach at last, I moved my hand towards it, only for it to be lifted by a human looking hand. I closed my eyes in defeat, too exhausted to care about what came next.

My eyes fluttered open as I smelled blood, and my tongue flicked out and tasted the O-negative. The packet was being held to my mouth, having been ripped open at the top. I stole it from the hand that held it and squeezed it down my throat, gulping greedily, at a rate that would appear to an outsider as if I'd been without fluid for centuries, not one day.

Finally sated, and realising I'd been held upright by sturdy hands, I smelled the wolf responsible for feeding me—Kellan. I collapsed back as the blood began to swim through me, revitalising every cell of my body and that's when it dawned on me that Kellan's clothes were still on the floor outside of the cell. Which, unless I'd blacked out and he'd decided to change into a new fresh look for the rest of the evening meant...

He was entirely naked behind me.

Chapter 9

KELLAN

I reached the doorway, expecting dust to coat both Nala and I, but it didn't. The stake landed to the right of Snow's heart. However, I couldn't tend to my captive as I had a wolf who'd gone rogue and needed reminding of her position within this pack. Grabbing Nala by the hair, I dragged her out of the cell. By the time we were both outside it, we'd both turned completely wolf.

Nala fought me, and we snapped and snarled at one another, fur flying, until she escaped my claws and retreated. We circled each other and my eyes narrowed on her. I prodded at her mind, and she dropped her guard, allowing me to speak to her telepathically.

Why the fuck did you try to kill her?

I didn't, she replied. *I intended to cause her extreme*

pain while weak to get her to talk. We're getting nowhere, Kellan, and in the meantime your father's killer is either still at large, or here with us.

It was not your place to make that decision. You should have spoken to me about it.

You'd have refused.

As is my right as alpha. Once more, you have forgotten your new position in the pack. I know this is difficult for you. I know how much you loved my father. But we handle this my way now I'm the alpha. Get out of here and think about your actions. We will talk more on this tomorrow. It goes without saying that you are banned from my house and from going anywhere near Snow.

Nala stopped pacing, raised her head, and opened her mouth like she would howl down the room. I took a step towards her, slamming down my right paw.

How can you not want to do anything you can to avenge your father? she asked. *Where is your grief, your emotion? Instead, you pussyfoot around this vampire woman like she's made of what she's named after. She's a killer. Watch out because snow can freeze and then it's treacherous.*

*I said **leave**.*

Very well. We shall speak tomorrow.

Returning to her human self, Nala gathered up what she could of her clothes, quickly dressed, and left.

Meanwhile, I made my way over to the cell to see what had become of Snow. I saw the stake now laid on the ground, surrounded by a small pool of blood. Snow was pulling herself across the floor slower than a sloth, as she reached for the packet of blood.

I didn't think beyond helping her. I picked up the packet, and sat behind Snow, pulling her fatigued body between my legs and holding her upright. I tore the packet with my teeth and fed the blood to her. The moment she began to respond to the blood, she took the packet from me and fed hungrily.

When finished, she let the packet fall from her hands and then slumped against me.

A feeling of heaviness sunk through my body, alongside a tightness in my chest. We'd so far uncovered no evidence of Snow's guilt and she'd almost lost her life because of one of my pack. My previous hatred of all vampires was being challenged by the individual in the cell. What if some vampires were actually good? What if she was one of them? I felt deep shame. My father had trained me in being the next alpha all my life, but I couldn't help thinking I was fucking this up big time.

"Are you fucking naked?" Snow suddenly yelled,

leaping away from me and bringing me out of my thoughts.

She turned around and her eyes flitted to my cock.

"Ew, ew, ew. Put it away," she screeched.

I shook my head in disbelief, my upper lip quirking. One moment Snow was near death, the next she was jumping around like the floor had springs.

"That's not the usual response I get when a woman sees my dick," I drawled. "Anyway, you're welcome for me helping save your life."

"It's your fault I'm in here and vulnerable in the first place!" she snapped, hands on her hips, and an incredulous look on her face. She headed for the door of the cell which was open. I leaped up and blocked the exit with my hands. Snow's body careered into mine.

"Ewwww. Now I can feel it next to my thigh. Get away from me," she shrieked.

"My apologies, but no one said you could leave."

"I was going to get your clothes," she retorted, every word getting louder. "So I don't have to look at your dick."

Rather than annoy me, her haughty tone made me snigger. "I'll go get them myself. You stay there. We need to talk some more," I said, walking backwards to my clothes on purpose so my cock swung around.

"You're disgusting."

"I don't trust having my back to you. By the way, you're still looking," I pointed out. "You could turn away your gaze at any time."

"I just survived being staked. Forgive me if I don't wish to turn my back on you either."

"Wolves are oftentimes naked, Snow," I pointed out.

Her eyes narrowed. "You're loving this. Who knew that flashing me was how the moody alpha would show an emotion."

And just like that, I shut down. I was not acting like an alpha. I was acting like an idiot. I quickly dressed.

"Do you think I might get a change of clothes, only this jacket and my t-shirt now have a hole in them," Snow remarked.

"We'll discuss that when I've asked you the questions I originally came in here to ask," I said. I left the cell door open, but I took the seat in front of it and Snow sat back down on her chair. You wouldn't have known she'd just been staked. The blood had completely restored her.

You're staring at her.

I took the phone from my pocket.

"You have messages and I need to know how to reply," I stated.

"Read them," she said simply.

She dictated a reply to Iris that she was enjoying Pladstone and staying an extra night. Then she had me send a message to her mother that everything was okay, and she hoped they were enjoying the holiday.

Her mother quickly replied that they were, but she missed her. The message made me think of my own mother and how I missed her too.

"Your mum says, 'call soon'."

"Tell her I will when I get the chance, but I'm busy enjoying the silence."

I sent the text.

"She says 'ha ha'."

"Thought she would." Snow smiled a wistful smile.

"Come on," I said, suddenly having a change of plans.

"What?"

"I'm taking you to my bedroom." I realised how that sounded as soon as I said it.

"You are *not*." Snow wrinkled her nose.

"Hear me out, okay? I have an enormous… walk in shower. You can get clean and change into some of your other clothes. Then we talk, and if I'm satisfied with your responses, you're free to go."

"Seriously?" She stood completely still. "Why the change of heart?"

"I can do better than I have," I said simply.

"I'm not going to argue with you when it means I get a shower and to brush my teeth."

"Come on." I gestured with a nod of my head, and together we walked outside of the room. I was on guard though. One attempt at escape and Snow would be back inside that cell and this time I wouldn't go easy on her. I'd decided that by giving her a little freedom, if she was complicit, she would make a move.

Ace, Pierce, Diego, Trent, and Samuel were in the living room. They all looked at me and then at Snow. She did a little wave. "Hey, guys," she said.

They all muttered responses of hello back, but their eyes gave away their true feelings on her being out of the cell. Either filled with disproval or confusion.

"What's happening, Boss? Nala shot out of here and wouldn't speak to any of us," Trent enquired.

"There was an incident. One which has had me reconsidering my position on things. Snow is going to get showered and changed and then we'll all sit together. I'll inform you of what just occurred and then we'll talk to Snow. Where's Tommo?" I asked.

"In the bedroom with Raina," Ace informed me.

My eyes widened. "Seriously?" I'd not seen that one coming.

"Seems she's got the message, Boss."

"Good," I replied, though I highly doubted it. I turned to Snow who raised a brow. "Let's go." I nodded in the direction of the stairs.

She followed me without hesitation.

I allowed no one in my bedroom suite. It was the place I could have total privacy. I'd thought the first woman to enter this space would be my mate, but instead it had turned out to be a vampire.

Snow's eyes flicked quickly around the room. At the enormous bed, the large space in front of it adorned with many blankets, the simple furniture. I pointed towards the door in front of us to the right. "Bathroom's in there." I picked up her backpack that I'd left on the end of my bed and handed it to her. "If there's anything of mine you need to use, towels etc, feel free."

"Thanks," she said and without a further word she walked away and into the bathroom. I followed her in just as she threw her jacket on the floor.

"What are you doing?" she asked.

"I need to make sure you don't try any funny business. Behind that shower curtain you have privacy, but I'm not closing a door on you."

"Whatever," she said. "You can pass me a towel when I'm done." She climbed into the shower, making sure the curtain was covering her from me and then I heard the rustling of clothes. She threw them out of the side of the curtain, and then I heard the shower turn on.

I sat on the toilet seat while I waited, resting my back against the tiles of the bathroom wall, my hands behind my head. Closing my eyes, I thought of my father, but my memories were now sullied. All I could see when I closed my eyes were body parts in a box.

Who the fuck was responsible for this?

"If there is a God, please help me," I whispered. "I don't know what to do next."

My head spun with a million thoughts and ruminations. Had I handled the situation with Snow properly? Was I being taken for a fool, and she was an accomplice to our enemy? Over and over, I thought the same damn thoughts to the point where I just wanted to knock myself out so I could have some peace.

"Can I have that towel now please?" Snow said after around five minutes. I passed her a large bath towel and heard her dry herself off. "Now my bra, a fresh pair of panties, and my white dress please."

I passed those through one at a time.

"I'll leave the door open and wait in my room," I told her.

A minute later Snow walked out of the room smelling of my shower gel. She wore the long white dress with a tan belt around the middle and was towelling her long, dark hair.

She came and sat at the end of the bed and licked her top teeth with her tongue.

"Erm," she began.

"Yes?"

"I have really powerful hearing," she said. "I heard your plea for help and advice."

"Oh."

"Pierce told me that your father was murdered. I'm so sorry, Kellan."

I kept my face impassive. "Are you? Or are you in fact in on the murder?"

She sighed. "I don't know what else I can do or say. We're going around in circles." She went in her backpack and brought out a brush. After detangling her hair, she beckoned me off the bed. "Come with me a moment," she ordered. "Into the bathroom."

I huffed. "Why?"

"Humour me."

With a sigh, I got up and followed her.

"Even though you were in here with me. If I wanted to, I could have left," she said.

I scoffed. "How?"

She climbed back into the shower and closed the curtain.

"Meet me downstairs," she said.

Then it went quiet. I pulled back the shower curtain and she was gone. I looked at the plughole. She couldn't have gone down there, surely? Then I saw the bathroom window. It was locked open, with only a few inches of room. But it was enough for a small creature to fly through.

So vampires did become bats. I'd thought that was all a myth.

However, just like when I became a wolf, Snow's clothes were discarded on the bathroom floor. Grabbing them, I raced downstairs so I could reach her before the other wolves did.

As I appeared, the others got up from their seats. "What's happening? Has she escaped?" they panicked.

"Stay seated," I yelled, opening the door, and finding Snow's head peeking out from behind a tree.

"I didn't think this entirely through," she said.

I started laughing. It was just what I needed in this

time of uncertainty. Whether Snow was good or evil, she was a revelation, that was for sure. I threw her clothing next to the tree. "Come back in when you're ready. Do vampires like hot drinks?"

"This vampire would like a hot tea with a shot of scotch if you have it," she replied.

"I have it."

I went inside and left the door open.

Chapter 10

SNOW

I came back inside to find Kellan had gone to the liquor cabinet. Then he walked in the direction of what I assumed was the kitchen.

Going to follow him, I found my arm being snagged by Ace. "Come sit with us, Snow, and tell us what's been happening."

He dropped his grip as he stopped speaking and I looked for a space on the sofas among the others. Ace and Diego moved up to create a gap in the middle for me.

Ohhhkayyyy. Hot guy sandwich it was.

I squashed myself in between them. Vampire males were slim but strong with cord-like sinew. These wolves were built like giant rugby players. Their thighs were so wide they should each have a capital city. My own thighs edged against theirs. I felt so slight at the side of them, but the heat from their bodies felt nice against my naturally cold state.

"Okay, spill. We don't have any patience when it comes to gossip," Diego said.

"Nala staked me but missed. Kellan felt bad and let me shower. Then I escaped to show I could. Think that's it," I stated.

"That is not it," the man himself replied, walking back in with a tray carrying my hot tea, a bottle of scotch and six glasses.

He unscrewed the lid off the scotch bottle and turned to me, "Say when," he ordered, beginning to pour the liquid.

"When," I answered after a hefty tipple had hit the tea.

He poured scotch into the other glasses and then walked to the bottom of the staircase, bellowing. "Tommo, get the fuck down here. We have urgent pack business to discuss."

My eyes met those of the other wolves.

"How did you get outside?" Samuel asked me.

"Turned into a bat and escaped through the window. Just to show the boss I could. Now he's even more confused as to my innocence." I wiggled my brows.

"But why didn't you escape if you had the chance?" Samuel added, confused.

"Because Kellan would come after me anyway," I said.

"Damn straight," Kellan replied, sitting down on the third sofa beside Pierce.

Soft voices came from the top of the stairs: a male and a female. I could make out that he was asking if he could see her again later, and she was flirting back in agreement. I watched as Tommo walked down; a blonde woman clung to his arm. She fawned all over him as they reached the living room, but her eyes kept checking on Kellan. I tried to read her mind, but her shields were firmly in place. She clearly felt my attempt as her gaze swung to me.

"Hey!" she said, leaving Tommo's side and walking over, holding out a hand. "I'm Raina."

I took it and shook back, surprised by the friendly response. "Snow," I replied.

"I thought you were imprisoned in the time out room?" she queried.

"Time to leave, Raina," Kellan ordered.

She turned to him and nodded. "Okay, Kel. Call

me when you're free again, Tommo," she said in a husky voice, walking back up to him and fixing her mouth on his, kissing him passionately. Then she winked at Kellan and walked out.

"You know she's trying to make 'Kel' jealous, mate?" Ace addressed Tommo.

"Course. But she's a mighty fine fuck, and you know, Kellan's made it clear he's not interested. She'll come around, and if not, I'll enjoy it while it lasts."

"Apologies for the pig-like behaviour of Tommo," Pierce said to me.

"Take me or leave me." Tommo shrugged his shoulders and sat down beside Samuel, grabbing a scotch on the way. He had that stereotypical rock star look about him, with shaggy brown hair, stubble, and looking like he'd only just got home from an all-nighter.

Kellan then proceeded to tell them about what had happened with Nala.

"She didn't actually want to kill me?" My mouth hung open. It felt plausible, but of course she'd say that to cover her tracks, wouldn't she?

"Apparently not, but I don't think it's worth the risk of having her anywhere near you," Kellan said. He took my phone from his pocket. "Now if I can just ask you a question about some messages I found on here."

I took a sip of my tea while I waited. The heat of the tea and then the burn of the whisky were much welcomed.

"You've messaged someone you have under the entry of 'gym', as in gymnasium," he began, and I felt my body go taut. Kellan noticed it too. "Didn't think it was a personal trainer," he said. "You wanted to meet this person urgently. For what reason?"

"For a personal reason," I replied.

"That's not good enough. Are you on drugs, Snow? I mean it could be a nickname because you like the white stuff. Did this person agree to supply you if you did them a little delivery job in return?"

I folded my arms across my chest. "Have you ever thought of being a writer? Your imagination is astonishing."

"Then tell me what the truth is, and I won't have to make shit up," he demanded.

"No." I was firm with my answer. I saw Kellan's nostrils flare and his eyes flashed yellow in warning.

The other wolves looked among one other, and I saw Diego smirk across at Pierce. Unfortunately, Kellan saw it too. The next thing I knew I was off my feet and being pinned against the wall by an alpha wolf. I'd disrespected him in front of his council. He was now showing me my place.

"You'll tell me what that message is about, or you'll go back in that cell, and this time I will not bring you food until you answer," he snarled, loud enough for his pack mates to hear.

The heat of his body burned through mine as he pinned me in place, and the fury in his gaze made me give in. I wasn't ashamed of my needs, so they could all hear them.

"It's a fellow vampire named Andre. He meets me in secret."

Those eyes went amber, and a small growl came from Kellan's throat.

"A fuck buddy?"

"No. A fight buddy."

Kellan let me go and stood back a step. "A what?"

"I like to feel pain. When I get the urge, Andre meets me at a derelict building. We fight until I've had enough and then I wait to heal and return home. My family wouldn't understand."

"You meet a guy in secret so he can smack you around?" Kellan's tone fucked me right off. He wasn't getting it at all.

"No. I do it because it suits my vampiric nature. I can't sit all day in my ivory tower being a good daughter when inside me I'm naturally a hunter, prey driven. With Andre, I can let that side out. I can taunt him and attack him, and he retaliates within limits so that at the end of the session I'm satisfied; my true nature feels like it's had a workout. That's why he's under gym, because to me he is my equivalent of a personal trainer. Without him I'd either go insane, or I worry I'd actually lose my humanity and hurt someone." My voice broke. "Do you understand what I'm saying? I'm not some scared woman who's being smacked around by her husband without her consent. I know what I need, and I seek it."

Kellan stood mute, staring down at me. His body was rigid, his lips a white slash.

And then he backed away from me.

"Thank you for answering my questions," he stated as if he hadn't just dragged me halfway across the room.

He walked back to the sofa and after a moment to recollect myself, I followed him.

Kellan addressed me in front of the others. "I don't see any further reason for me to keep you here. There's no indication of any involvement with what's happening to us. If the others agree, you're free to leave. Though we will keep an eye on you just in case."

The first thing I noticed was that Pierce and Ace

looked disappointed, though everyone agreed with him that there was no reason to keep me captive.

I could return to Moonstone, but for some reason that now didn't seem as exciting as it did before my family went on holiday. I could carry on and do a little travelling, seeking new and safer adventures… but until they found their enemy, the wolves would watch me anyway.

I might as well stay where I was.

"Thanks, but I'll stay a bit longer if that's okay," I said.

Kellan splattered out his whisky. "*What?*"

The others also stared at me, mixed emotions flittering across their features while they waited for an explanation. Pierce was smiling, Tommo was scowling, and the others looked confused.

"My dad told me I needed to see a bit of the world. Now I know he meant maybe taking in the sights of the major cities, but I've ended up here, and to be truthful I find you wolves interesting. You've said you're going to keep tabs on me if I leave anyway, so I might as well stay and see if I can help with finding out who your enemy is." I offered a small smile. "You're convinced they're a vampire. I might be able to confirm or deny that. If it's okay with you, I'd like to stay as a guest, for a day or so. That means getting my belongings back." I gestured for Kellan to hand me my phone by holding out my hand, palm up.

Rather than lean over to place it there, he threw it across at me. Of course, with my natural instincts I caught it effortlessly.

"If you could give us a moment, I need to discuss this with the others," Kellan said. Then he sighed. "You'll hear us anyway, won't you?"

I shook my head. "Not if I take myself upstairs. I'll go back to your room. Let me know when you've made your decision." Rising from the sofa, I left them all to discuss my fate and walked upstairs.

The room smelled overwhelmingly of Kellan. Of his natural musk, his deodorant and aftershave. It mixed in with the smell of the cabin: creating a combination that was woody and masculine. I breathed it all in. I didn't 'breathe' as in needing to do so to live, but I inhaled smells, and often liked to sigh for emphasis so sometimes an intake of air was useful.

After thinking about leaving and potentially travelling on, I'd quickly decided that I was already somewhere I'd like to explore more. I'd not been in their woodland, not seen how the pack as a whole lived.

Perhaps it was a dumb idea. If so, it would quickly be thrown out by the wolves, and then I would leave. If that happened, I decided I would return home and then I'd do some fact finding and make a plan about where I'd like to travel next. When Kellan had judged me for seeking pain, he'd reminded me of what most people's opinions of it would be. The thought of my family and the local townspeople judging me made my shoulders lock with tension. But there was a whole world out there and maybe there was someplace where what I needed was the norm. I couldn't be the only vampire driven almost to insanity by their natural instincts not being used enough.

Andre was already tired of fighting me and not fucking me. My options at home were running out. I wondered if my sprinting through the woods with the wolves might help, and I genuinely wanted to see if I could offer any fresh insights into who had murdered Kellan's father. He might try to hide his feelings and pretend he was like cold, hard granite, but I could see below that surface. The alpha was also a man. One who'd lost his father, and who needed to mourn, but held it all in to keep his pack strong.

That wasn't healthy and soon Kellan would snap.

I might come from an overprotective family, whereas Kellan now only had his pack, but we weren't so dissimilar when it came to our natures. We were both natural hunters and yet people who cared deeply. Maybe I could offer a shoulder? Be an impartial person to talk to?

Plus, if they let me stay a day or so, I'd have a chance to get to know the others. My first impressions of the other wolves had been favourable and that was when they'd figured I could be their enemy. How would it go if they saw me as a potential friend?

I think you're living in a fantasyland, Snow, I told myself. *Just go home.*

I heard the tread of heavy footfall on the stairs, and the smell of Kellan's scent came ever closer. He knocked on the door before opening it and walking in.

He scrubbed a hand through his hair. "I have absolutely no clue why you've asked to stay. Not really. I kept you in a cell for God's sake. But the others are happy for you to stay as a guest, and I accept your offer of help in looking over the evidence of our enemy. There's only one condition I have, and I know you'll not like it."

"Oh yeah?"

"There must always be one of us nearby. That's for your safety. We can be downstairs, but there must always be someone in the house with you, or if you go outside, accompanying you."

"That's not a problem at all."

"That's not the condition, that's just an instruction."

"Oh, so what's the condition?" I waited.

"You sleep in my room," he said.

Chapter 11

Kellan

I carried on. "I have the large area in front of the bed where I mainly sleep. I prefer it to the bed anyway. So the bed would be yours, and I'd either be outside of the room, or I'd sleep in front of the bed on the blankets. This is to ensure your safety. That's not a debatable point if you stay. Sorry."

"And you definitely sleep on those blankets at the foot of the bed as a rule and aren't just saying that to make me feel better about taking your bed?" she asked.

"It's the truth. Now I prefer to slumber in my wolf form, but if that makes you uncomfortable, I'll stay like this. Our sleep will only overlap for a few hours anyway."

She shrugged her shoulders nonchalantly. "I have

no problem with you being a wolf. Please don't do anything differently on my account."

I rubbed the back of my neck. "Why do you want to stay, Snow? I thought you'd whizz out of here and back home before I could blink." I said this in a quiet tone. The woman had completely confused me when she'd made her request.

Snow didn't reply for a moment.

"Can you come and sit beside me on the edge of the bed?" she requested eventually. "You looming over me being so enormous is really off-putting."

I smirked. I couldn't help it.

She rolled her eyes. "Please don't tell me you're smirking because I said enormous and you're thinking of your dick again. Can it just be because you're preening over your huge frame."

"I'm being a cocky alpha. Take that anyway you like," I joked as I made my way over to the bed. I made sure to sit down gently as it wasn't my natural state to be delicate about things.

"I know my request seems strange, but I want to stay because it's an opportunity I'm unlikely to ever get again," she answered.

I raised a brow.

"I've lived such a sheltered life that I've never met a wolf before. How you and the others bond like brothers is so incredible, and also..." she hesitated, and her mouth opened then closed.

"Say it. Whatever it is."

"I thought I might run with the pack, if you do that. I've read you do. It might help me burn off this energy I have without feeling I have to fight or be thrown at walls."

"So not only do you want to find out more about us, you're wondering if it might also help answer some questions within yourself?"

She nodded her head emphatically. "Yes, that's exactly it. And also, if I can help in any way to find out who killed your father, that would please me."

"Why? If you're not involved in his murder, then why would you want to get involved?"

"Because I know you're hurting and if I left without seeing if I could do anything, well, that wouldn't sit right with me."

"I'm fine."

"Is that why you flinched when I mentioned my vampire father tearing you limb from limb? Such a visceral reaction to my kind indicated to me that you were anything but fine. I'm an outsider, talk to me. It doesn't matter if you're vulnerable with me. I'll be gone in a couple of days."

I didn't know how she managed it, but if I had

buttons, she sure would be pushing every one of them firmly with one of those long, slim fingers.

"The black box found at the side of you contained my father's tongue. Before that I'd received his heart, his head, and his hands," I confessed.

Snow's own hand flew across her mouth. She blinked rapidly, staring at me in utter horror. "Th-that's despicable. Oh my god, Kellan, I'm so sorry. And I said my father would tear you limb from limb. No wonder you had such a reaction. I don't know how you kept so calm and didn't tear my throat out. I am so, very, very sorry I said that."

"You weren't to know." I knew this now. Leaving maybe a one percent chance I could be wrong, I otherwise felt deep in my bones that Snow was not part of what had happened to my father.

"I'm still sorry anyway. Please do take me up on my offer of help." Her hand rubbed up and down her breastbone.

"Pierce is going through the evidence again. Maybe you could assist him with that?"

"Absolutely." Her face changed in response to me mentioning Pierce. I'd seen their secret smiles. I'd seen how all the rest of the wolves had reacted to Snow. In fact, there was no time like the present, while they were all still downstairs, for me to place some ground rules about their behaviour around our guest.

"I'd like to cook for you all while I'm here, and maybe do a little tidying up?" Snow enquired.

"That won't be necessary. I mean, you don't even eat."

"I can enjoy the taste of food, alongside my quota of O-neg. Please, Kellan. It would make me feel more comfortable. At home, I'm always helping out, being the oldest of six."

"You have five siblings?"

"Well, duh, if I'm the oldest of six."

Again with the smart comeback. "You know what I mean. Brothers or sisters?"

"The two eldest after me are sisters, and then I have three brothers. I'm twenty, Dove is nineteen, Isabel eighteen. Then there's Phillipe at seventeen, Gene sixteen, and Reid who's the youngest at fifteen."

"Ah, yes. Vampire males are fertile for five years at a time."

"Yes," she confirmed. "And this was my father's first nest of children, though he says he doesn't feel the need to have any more."

"He might feel different when his fertility hits the second time," I said.

Snow shrugged. "What about wolves? Pierce told

me his mother is nagging him to reproduce. As the alpha are you under pressure to carry on the line?"

"I don't have a mother to nag me like Pierce does. Mine died in a car crash when I was a teenager." I didn't add that I'd been in the car at the time. It was another thing I kept buried deep within me.

Snow looked at me with sympathy. "You must miss her terribly."

"I miss both my parents, but life goes on, and I've a pack I'm responsible for." That was enough chatter for one day. For some reason this woman seemed to have ways of getting me to speak. While it eased the pain furrowed into my chest, it also made me feel vulnerable, and that wasn't something I was comfortable with.

"Please excuse me. I must go speak with the others before they leave. Feel free to do what you wish within my prior instructions. It's not safe out there. Someone killed my father and they hurt you. I don't want your father visiting me because you've been hurt... or worse." My mind flashed to receiving Snow's head in a box. The red ribbon placed in her hair instead of around the outside of the box. I shuddered.

I felt her eyes upon me and met her gaze. Saw the sympathy still there. Urgently requiring distance between us, I excused myself and returned downstairs to the others.

Sharing Snow

My roommates had stayed on the sofas waiting to be dismissed. I sat back down among them.

"Back to our previous plans. We continue to monitor the woods and the perimeters. Pierce, Snow has agreed to check through all the evidence with you to see if she spots something we've missed. Tommo, can I leave it with you to organise a rota of perimeter checks etc?"

"Of course," Tommo said.

"I'll make a plan." Pierce looked altogether too happy about the prospect of spending time with Snow and a tight feeling coiled deep in the pit of my stomach. It was a strange sensation I'd not experienced before, like a snake lived in my belly and was letting itself be known. Was it jealousy? My stomach grumbled, giving me the excuse to dismiss it as nothing but hunger. That's what I told myself, refusing to look beyond the surface.

"I think we still need to keep a close eye on our guest, just in case she's playing us," Tommo stated. A couple of the others nodded their agreement.

"Absolutely," I also agreed. "I've told her she must have one of us in the house with her at all times and be accompanied if she goes out. It's not only for her own safety, but also because I don't want a woman who we barely know at liberty to do what she likes in our territory." Obviously, I'd not told Snow I still couldn't one hundred percent trust her. "The other thing I must ask is that none of you try to take advantage of our guest in a sexual way." I gazed around at them all. "She's an adult and if anything consensual takes place that's on you. Just remember we don't know her, and that she's currently a guest."

"We don't have to remain celibate while she's here, do we? My balls will burst," Trent said dramatically.

"You carry on however you see fit. Snow wants to see what the pack's like, so let her see what the pack's like. If she doesn't like your playtimes, she can go sit in my room out of the way."

"So it's okay to pursue something with her if she's amenable?" Ace asked, as I'd suspected one of them might.

"Knock yourselves out," I said.

"And if she says no, just think of her and knock one out instead," Trent joked.

I groaned. "Get out of here all of you," I said. "Oh, Snow also said she'd like to cook for us."

"Is that because she knows the rules about if we cook for her?" Diego queried.

Cooking for a female meant we were showing

them our interest in claiming them for a mate.

"Probably wants to lace our steak with poison," Tommo noted. I needed to officially make this guy my deputy, because while he could appear pessimistic, he was an extra voice of reason.

"I believe it's because she wants something to do and to be useful. If you're all okay with us sitting down to eat together tonight, she can cook this evening. But we will err on the side of caution at all times. Actually, you can supervise her," I told Tommo. "Frisk her before she enters the kitchen for all I care. Samuel, you sort the perimeter checks now that Tommo's otherwise engaged."

"Can I stay and frisk her instead?" Trent joked.

"Yeah, we need someone who won't be hypnotised if she flashes you a nipple," Tommo teased.

"I'm going to go to the gym now. Anyone else coming?" I asked, eager to get out of here for a while.

"Yeah, I'll come with you, Boss," Pierce said eagerly.

I nodded, though inside I wanted to scream. I had a feeling that Pierce wanted to talk to me some more about personal relations with Snow, whereas I wanted to get to the gym and pound out the day. One time I might get to go there and leave all the shit behind.

But today was clearly not that day.

"Have shifters and vampires ever got together before?" Pierce asked me, not a moment after we left the cabin.

"Sure. It doesn't usually last though. The species are too different."

"But it does happen?" he re-iterated.

"Yes. Nala's ex was a vampire. They had a child together, but he favoured the father. Had no wolf in him at all as far as she could make out. The only thing she noticed was when angry, her son's eyes flashed red, but if truly in a temper they turned yellow."

"I didn't know Nala had a son."

"Don't mention I've told you about it either. Her ex thought she'd have a litter of children. When she only birthed one, he decreed she was unsuitable and left, taking their son with him. Then she met my father and fell madly in love. My dad said she made the ultimate sacrifice to not seek out her son, knowing he was better off raised as a vampire."

"Wow. That must have been torture."

I'd never given much thought to Nala's past as her present had been so entwined with my father's. Did she think of this son now that her husband had gone?

"I guess. Anyway, back to your question. You're interested in pursuing things with Snow?"

Pierce looked at the floor. "Yes, I like her."

"You know Ace likes her too?"

He nodded and then said something that made my head spin.

"Actually, we all like her. Even Tommo."

"All of you?" I repeated. "So Snow's basically got a wolf buffet to choose from if she wishes?" My back prickled at the thought that Snow had seemingly charmed all of my roommates. Was she able to enthral them after all?

"Not necessarily. When I chatted with Snow, we both agreed that a person could love more than one person at the same time."

They did? When did they have such an intimate conversation?

"Just tread carefully, Pierce. We already have at least one enemy vampire. Please don't have Snow's family coming for us too."

"I won't," he said, just as we reached the gym. "Actually. Boss. I'm not feeling up to a workout after all. I'm going to head back to the cabin."

I should have felt relief that I was left in peace after all, but that niggle was back. They wanted Snow. Did she want them?

And why had I started to care?

Chapter 12

Snow

I would need to phone my mother and Iris shortly, but it was the last thing I felt like undertaking at present. There'd been so much sitting and talking, and now I felt like doing. But had the wolf business concluded so I could leave the room?

My question was answered when I heard a different sounding set of footsteps coming up the stairs and the scent of Tommo drifted underneath the door. I pulled open the door just as he'd raised his hand to knock.

My nostrils flared at the fact that up close he smelled of sex. Of course, being ordered downstairs by Kellan meant the guy hadn't had time to take a shower after getting it on with Raina.

"Is there something wrong?" he asked, backing away a little.

I shook my head. "I was just wondering if I was able to leave the room."

"Ah. That's why I'm here actually. Kellan asked me to show you around the kitchen. Apparently, you're wanting to cook?"

"I'd like to make myself useful."

"Have you ever fed seven hungry wolves before? It's not easy. We get *very* hungry and take some filling." He smiled. "We won't be offended if you change your mind."

"Well, I've not fed seven hungry wolves before, but I have fed eight vampires. We don't always just have blood. Sometimes it's nice to partake in a meal just to simply enjoy the flavours," I explained. "Also, family time is very important to us, so we sit down together a lot, even if just to have our blood."

"It would be nice to enjoy a meal together for once," Tommo admitted. "We've got into the habit of eating on the go of late, and at different times. Just know that our portion sizes are large. You'll be surprised when you see what we eat in one sitting."

"I can imagine. You must have a hefty food bill."

"Come on then. Let's go show you where everything is kept," he said.

Leaving the room and closing Kellan's door behind me, I followed Tommo down the stairs and through to the kitchen.

"The dining room is the next room along. I'll show you that next."

Tommo seemed friendly enough, but there was something else there. An edge. I got the feeling that he wasn't as happy as some of the others at my being here.

"I know it's weird, me staying," I prompted. "I'm happy to leave if I make you uncomfortable."

Tommo paused, clenching his hands together in front of me. "My apologies if I seem a little guarded. But while we have no evidence our enemy is you; we have this unknown assailant—who we believe to be a vampire—taunting us. I'm still wary."

"That's understandable. I would be too. Like I said, I can leave if that would be better."

"The thing is, I'm already worried Kellan is taking too much on, trying to be the alpha when he just lost his father. Now he's letting you stay and making things even more complicated." He scrubbed a hand through his hair. "But then that's why he has us. In order to carry some of that weight for him, so all will work out, I'm sure."

"Tommo," I asked gently.

"Yes?"

"If I do need to leave at any point, just tell me. I'd truly value your honesty."

He nodded. "Your offer is appreciated. Now there's just one thing I need to do before I let you cook and you're not going to like it," he said.

"Oh."

"I need to search you to make sure you're not hiding anything to put in the meals."

My mouth fell open. I'd not expected that. Which was stupid because he'd just told me he was still wary of me.

"Go for it," I said. "What do you need me to do?"

"Just stand still."

Tommo brought his hands to the top of my head, and he ran his fingers through my hair, around the back of my neck, my ears. He went down each of my arms, and then stood closer, moving a hand down from my underarms to my waist.

"I need to check inside your bra," he said.

"Are you joking? I'm not sure I wish to cook for you now," I huffed.

"Well, I'd search you anyway, because maybe there's a reason you don't want me to see inside your bra," he teased.

"There is. You'll see my boobs."

"I'm just going to sniff, not look or touch. This is

simply wolf business. I'm making sure you're clean, so you don't try to kill one of us."

"I'm more likely to want to kill you after this humiliation," I retorted.

"I'll go quick, okay? Hold up your arms."

I did so. Tommo slipped my dress off my shoulders and quickly dropped his nose to near my breasts. He took deep inhales as he worked his way around the cups and edges of my bra. I felt relief as he turned his attention to my back because his closeness had threatened to make my nipples harden.

Then he was done, and he helped me pull the arms of my dress back up to cover me.

"Satisfied now?" I asked.

"I need to do your legs, and check inside your shoes," he said. Tommo carried on smoothing his hands over my thighs, my calves, my feet, and then he checked my shoes.

"All good?"

He stood up. "Open wide, I'm going to look inside your mouth next."

"Fuck's sake."

The more annoyed I got, the more amused Tommo did.

"You're not putting those fingers in my mouth. God knows where they've been."

"I'm just looking, don't worry."

Again, his proximity was too close, in my personal space. I could hear his deep breathing, note the rise and fall of his chest.

"Are we finally done?" I complained as he stepped away.

"Nope. One final thing. I need you to lift up the skirt part of your dress please. There are places you can hide things that I've not searched yet."

"You can't be serious?" I backed away.

"I'm deadly serious. This is not sexual, Snow. You want to cook for us. I have to make sure you're not an assassin. While I understand it's not pleasant, as far as I'm concerned Kellan should have strip searched you the moment he put you in the cell. He's checked your belongings, but he failed to check you."

"Do you have to… t-touch me?" I said weakly.

"No. I just need to sniff again. You can leave your panties on. It'll be over in a minute, I promise."

"O-okay." I lifted up my skirt and widened my stance.

Tommo dropped to his knees and his head moved to between my legs. He picked up the material at the edge of my pants and then placed his nose there and sniffed. I knew that despite my best efforts, my body shivered with his proximity to my core. Tommo quickly moved away, moving behind me, parting my butt cheeks and sniffing my hole.

Yeah, I was over this now.

"Are we done here?" I challenged.

"Yeah," he declared, rising back to his feet. "You're clean and my mouth is salivating at the thought of dinner, so you can most definitely stay."

"Gee, thanks," I muttered sarcastically.

Tommo showed me the plentiful larder, the refrigerator, how to work the oven etc. Then we moved onto the dining room, where he pointed out the sideboard that housed the tableware.

"Do you want me to assist?" he asked.

"No, I'm fine. You should take the opportunity to have a shower before dinner," I replied.

"Are you saying I smell? I showered this morning," Tommo remarked, sniffing his underarm.

"I have a very strong sense of smell and you've just been balls deep in Raina," I pointed out.

His mouth fell open. "You can smell *that*?"

"Yup, and while it's not unpleasant, it is quite distracting smelling your life juice and her lubrication."

"Life juice!" Tommo belly laughed, holding onto the wall with one hand as he doubled over. "Oh my goodness, Snow, you have such a way with words."

I shrugged. "You asked, and I'm telling you. So, shower?"

"I'm on my way," he said, walking out of the dining room, chuckling all the while.

While the meat was cooking, I whizzed around and set the table for eight of us. There was no one else around downstairs, so having found the vacuum cleaner, I vacuumed the carpets. Some elements of cooking—like chopping vegetables—I did at vampire speed, but I couldn't make the oven cook food any faster, so I busied myself with the housework in between.

Kellan returned an hour after he'd left, with damp hair, and smelling of endorphins. I wanted to sniff his skin. It was setting off that need in me. The need to run, to seek what could satisfy my craving, that 'itch' I found hard to scratch. After checking I was okay, he headed off upstairs to shower and change, and in response to my reaction to his scent, I flew around the downstairs at lightning speed, cleaning every surface, and mopping floors.

By the time I called everyone to take a seat at the table, the whole place gleamed. Every window sparkled, and I'd also lit some candles I'd found. I think the wolves kept them for in case of power cuts, but I placed four down the centre of the dining table.

I knew every bit of the cabin now—apart from the wolves' rooms and en-suites—like I'd lived here for years. Vampire speed and focus had proved useful, and it had also burned off some of that energy I'd wanted to release.

Until seven large, burly wolves entered the room, dressed in shirts and dress pants, smelling of pheromones and aftershave. It was a sensory overload and I thought I might actually pass clean out with the processing and the lust that hit my system.

But then the wolves themselves sniffed the air. Oh my god. Of course, they'd be able to scent my arousal, wouldn't they?

I felt my cheeks bloom with heat, as hungry-eyed wolves stared at me. Until Kellan broke the silence.

"Wow, Snow, dinner smells so good, doesn't it, my brothers? Plus, take in setting of the dining room table. It looks amazing."

"We barely sit together here," Ace remarked. "We usually sit on the sofa in front of the television."

"Yeah, I guessed that with the dirt and crumbs that were under the sofas," I joked.

"You've worked hard, Snow," Samuel said. "Our

cabin looks like we've had a team of cleaners in. Thank you."

"Not a problem. I enjoyed doing it all. Now please, sit down and let me bring in the food before it gets cold."

"Would you like any of us to help?" Trent asked.

"No, I have it all in hand," I told him.

Being occupied on the delivery of food to the table, rather than focusing on how attractive all the men looked, thankfully helped my libido to calm down.

A few minutes later, the table was piled high with different sliced cooked joints of meat, silver servers filled with vegetables, and all the wolves had a drink of their choice: some beer, some water, some wine.

"Help yourself," I said.

All looked to Kellan.

"Please raise a glass," he ordered, doing so himself. "To our cook tonight, Snow. We thank you for all of the hard work you've put in this evening. We shall of course do the washing up."

"No, I'm happy to do it," I protested.

"To Snow," he repeated, ignoring me. Everyone joined in, and then with Kellan's approval they tucked into the food.

Within half an hour the table was empty of every morsel of food. They'd even had dessert. I'd found apple pies in the fridge and served them with large jugs of custard I'd found in the larder. The kitchen sink and worktops were piled with dishes, and I stood looking at the mess.

"That's why we'll do the dishes," Kellan said from behind me. "It's a large endeavour."

I couldn't help myself. Smirking at him, I employed vampire mode and dashed around. Within a couple of minutes everything was washed and stacked to air dry.

Kellan stood rubbing his forehead. "I tried to watch and went incredibly dizzy. You're a stubborn one, Miss..." his voice trailed off. "I don't even know your surname and I held you prisoner. There's no wonder I haven't found the murderer yet. My detective skills are dire."

"Salinger," I informed him. "Snow Raven Salinger."

He pondered over my name for a moment. "What a perfect name, for a woman who seems so very innocent, but actually is a vampire," he remarked eventually.

"What's your full name?" I asked him. "It's only fair you return the favour."

"Kellan Santos Luna," he replied, surprising me by offering the information so speedily. "My middle name is after my father. Our pack is named Luna, after my father and his father before him."

There was a pause then, Kellan sucking the left side of his top lip. I waited.

"Have you had sufficient 'exercise' with the housework, or do you need the time out room again?" he enquired.

"The cooking and cleaning have hit the spot, thank you. Tomorrow night though, if I'm still here, I'd like to run with some of you."

He nodded. "Then I'll bid you goodnight, Snow Raven Salinger. I'm on patrol this evening in the woods with Samuel. The others are around should you wish to keep them company."

"Actually, I need to go and speak with my mother," I stated. "Although if I could I'd try to avoid it."

Kellan smiled. "She loves you and just wishes to know you're safe," he said, walking out of the kitchen.

Which then seemed cavernous without him in it.

I finished drying the dishes with a tea-towel in the human way while I replayed the dinner in my mind. It had gone well, everyone appreciative of the meal I'd cooked. Something about this place just felt right when it should have felt anything but. I should have felt like a cuckoo in the nest, but instead I'd actually enjoyed the evening and the company. Finished, I left the kitchen myself. As I passed the sofa, Ace asked me if I was joining them to watch a movie.

"Maybe later. Right now, I just need to call my mum," I said with a grimace. I was more nervous of speaking to her than I was living with seven wolves.

There was clearly something seriously wrong with the logical side of my brain.

Chapter 13

Snow

I totally bailed on calling my mum and sent a message to my father asking him to call me.

Dad: Urgent?

Snow: Not to me, but you might feel differently.

Dad: Gimme five to come up with an excuse to escape them all.

Snow: Okay.

A few minutes later, my phone rang.

"Hey, Dad."

"Hey to you too. However, how come you want to

talk to me and not your mother? That's never a good sign. If I had a beating heart it would be thumping in my chest right now. Spill."

"Everything is fine. That's the first thing you need to know."

"Thank goodness for that. Are you enjoying your time alone?"

Here went nothing. "You're out of earshot of Mum, aren't you?"

"Yesssss..."

"Okay, so actually... I've been travelling around a little like you suggested, but it's not exactly gone to plan."

There was a silence where I knew that at the other end of this conversation, my father was probably ready to sprint to my side and give me a piece of his mind for lying.

"Where, sweet daughter, have you been, and where are you now?" His voice was laced with suspicion.

"I'm free now, but I... erm... got kidnapped."

"Kidnapped? KIDNAPPED? Snow Raven Salinger, this had better be a very inappropriate and very unamusing wind up," he yelled.

My silence confirmed to him that it was not.

"Tell me everything, right now," he demanded.

So I did.

"You did encourage me to explore some of the world while Mum wasn't around," I said, attempting to defend my actions.

"A fact that may just have me staked when I re-join her shortly," he muttered with heavy sarcasm. "Snow, I would rather you went home instantly."

"But I don't want to," I replied. "I'd like to stay a couple more days and see how they live and interact. It's interesting."

A large sigh came from the other side of the phone. "Call me on videocall immediately, so I can check you aren't there with a stake held next to your chest being forced to say this."

The fact I had been staked was something I'd chosen to leave out of the conversation, instead making my capture seem more of a misunderstanding.

I pressed end on the call and videocalled him. I'd never seen my father look so flustered as he paced while chatting.

"Show me the room you're in."

I scanned the room with the phone. "Kellan has given me his own suite, and they have wolves taking turns to watch me for my own safety. They are being very hospitable," I told him.

"That may be, but I need to speak with this alpha as soon as possible, Snow. Is he around?"

"Not at the moment. He's on surveillance duties."

"I'm not happy about the fact there is someone out for the pack while you're there. You've already ended up in a predicament because of it. It could be dangerous. What if this enemy captures you again?"

"Dad, I'm not going to be anywhere near them. I'm protected by seven wolves," I protested.

"As your father, I'm asking you one last time to consider returning home to the safety of Moonstone." He waited for my response.

I shook my head. "Sorry, Dad. I can't stay locked in the castle forever. I could be attacked on my way home from work. There are risks every day, and if we hide from the possibility, we're not living life, are we?"

It was funny how we still used the vernacular of life and living when we were undead. That thought made me smile.

"I don't know what you're finding so amusing. Is it the torment you're putting your poor father through? Your mother will be on the phone to you within seconds. You know that, right?"

Yup. But at least you'll have smoothed the way and taken some of the brunt of the blame." Now I did giggle.

Dad placed the phone down so that he could fold both arms across his chest. He glared into the camera.

"Your stay there is dependent on my conversation with the alpha. This is really testing all of my fatherly resolve, Snow. You're staying with seven male wolves. What if they try to take advantage of you?"

My dilating pupils must have given my thoughts away.

"Oh good lord, Snow." He shook his head as if trying to dislodge what he'd seen.

"I'm not planning on doing anything, Dad," I protested. "But I can't disguise the fact that they are all stunning godlike creatures."

"Can you please do compulsion on me and take away the last two minutes of our conversation," he begged.

"Dad, honestly, I'm just staying to learn more about pack life, and the wolves are protecting me."

"Snow, I am not happy with the fact you insist on staying there. However, if all appears well after discussion with the alpha, I will not stop you based on the fact you're an adult. But please, I beg, open your eyes. Wolves are particularly sexual creatures. They frolic in animal form and are extremely comfortable with nudity."

I tried hard not to think about Kellan's naked form, instead thinking about the chain that had been held around my neck and the violent punches I'd endured, to make my thoughts mirror my father's concerns.

"I know I have a father's bias, but, Snow, you are an exquisitely beautiful woman. To think that not even one of these wolves will find you attractive is quite frankly ridiculous. I'd rather not contemplate what could happen, but I have to be realistic. Be aware, and if you do decide to pursue anything, let it be known that your father will drain dry anyone who hurts you in the slowest, most painful way imaginable."

"I'm not pursuing anything," I protested. "I'm just going to spend time learning about the lives of wolves."

He sighed. "I must speak to this alpha at his earliest convenience. I shall however, now go and talk to your mother. Does Iris know where you are?"

"She believed I'd travelled to Pladstone, but I'd asked her to keep it to herself."

"She'll know the truth soon, so prepare for your godmother's wrath also."

"I have all night to talk to them both and no problem with doing so. Like you say, I'm an adult. Therefore, I should be able to move freely without having to give my co-ordinates to all."

"That might land better had you not been kidnapped."

"Ha ha," I said, sticking out my tongue, knowing full well he was right.

"Take care, my beautiful firstborn, and if you need me, I am but that whizz away from you."

"I know. Love you, Dad."

"Love you too, Snow. It's not easy watching my eldest daughter growing up, so please bear with me."

I smiled. "I'm just very grateful to have you, Dad. We're very lucky to have our close-knit family."

"It cannot be easy for the alpha, dealing with grief alongside running the pack," my father said astutely.

"I believe he does it by shutting the emotional side of himself down."

"Something I can understand. I had to do that when I sent your mother away."

"But you can't really avoid it, can you?" I prompted.

"You just busy yourself with other endeavours, Snow. But truthfully, in the times you find yourself alone in the quiet, the shadows of your sorrow seep into your very soul."

"Would you like to explain why you're hiding in the garden shed, husband, chatting away to our dear daughter?" my mother's voice sounded out, as she appeared behind him.

"And that's my cue to sign off. Your mother will

call you shortly," he said, and he reached forward for the phone and ended the call.

I laid back on the bed. So I had to get Kellan to speak to my dad. That wasn't a problem. What I couldn't believe was that my father had broached the possibility that the wolves might want to get hot and heavy with me. I felt my cheeks burn. What an excruciatingly embarrassing thing to talk about with my father.

Yet he'd opened up my mind to something I'd not allowed to come to the fore. My response to when the pack had come into the dining room. How I'd been aroused by how manly they were, how rugged. Right now, my pants dampened as I thought about each of them, finally settling on Kellan's naked form. Would I take the opportunity for sex if presented?

I had a feeling I probably would. My enquiring mind, my need to scratch this itch that I found no lasting answer to so far would tempt me to try new things. Then there was the fact that they shared women. I had no idea what that could possibly involve, but just the very thought excited me. Pulling the skirt of my dress up around my thighs, my hand edged under the waistband of my panties, where my finger found my pussy slick with arousal. I ran a finger through that wetness and knew that it wasn't going to take much for me to come. Closing my eyes, I imagined Pierce and Ace exploring my body, and I flicked at my clit. Within seconds I shook with my climax.

Shame immediately flooded my system, as I became aware of the fact I was laid on Kellan's bed with my hand in my panties, and I dashed to the shower in order to wash my cum away. I stayed under the shower for ages, washing myself with my sponge and shower gel over and over because if Kellan returned and scented what I'd done I'd be mortified.

When I finally left the bathroom, I saw my phone screen with five missed call notifications on it and a message from my mother.

Mum: Snow Salinger, call me IMMEDIATELY. Are you avoiding my call or dead?

I was so tempted to text back that of course I was dead but didn't feel my mother would appreciate the humour.

I dried myself off and returned her call, video-calling so we could speak face-to-face.

"Sorry, Mum. I was in the shower," I explained.

"You took a shower knowing I would be calling the

moment I heard what you were doing? And Iris is in trouble for not telling me you'd even left the house."

"I was trying to avoid you worrying about me."

"Congrats on that, with you going out and getting kidnapped. I only had a little apprehension before, but now I have a mountain of concern. We're coming home, and we'll collect you on the way."

"No, we're not," Dad shouted in the background.

"Even if you did come home, Mum, I'm not. So stay there and enjoy the rest of your holiday. I'm staying here for a couple of days. You are free to call me whenever you like to check I'm safe, but I'm twenty years old and you'll just have to... suck it up."

"Is that supposed to be a vampire joke? I'm not sharing your amusement right now, missy."

My posture slumped, my chin dipping as guilt hit. Mum was just worried about me, and I was trying to joke my way out of things. "Sorry, Mum. I know I've caused you some distress, but I'm fine, and you have to accept my decision. I'm staying. You were younger than me when you first went to the Lakes and to Paris, remember?"

She sighed as the truth of my words hit. "I'm not happy, and I will be calling you frequently to ensure you're okay. Is this alpha not back yet, because I'll feel better when we've had a chance to speak to him."

"Not yet, but as soon as he is, I'll ask him to call."

"Very well," Mum said, the fight going out of her. I could see she was on the cusp of weeping, and I couldn't deal with that right now. She swallowed a couple of times. "I love you, Snow."

"Love you too, Mum," I said, and we ended the call.

Chapter 14

Kellan

My surveillance shift finished at two am and Samuel and I were replaced by Trent and Diego. It had been a long day and a large yawn escaped me, confirming the fact I needed to rest. But would I be able to sleep with a female vampire in the room? And should I even risk it. What if she had caught us all in a very clever trap and tonight decided to split me into jigsaw pieces?

The truth—though I didn't want to admit it, not even to myself—was that part of me didn't care. If it weren't for my brothers, I'd have no one I called family around me, and my entire existence was focused around being the alpha. I had no time to grieve. No time to have a pity party. No real existence outside of my role as alpha anyway. The only person who was pecking at the protective shell I placed around me was the very person who could possibly have murdered my father in the first place. But what would she have to gain from it? My gut instinct was she was innocent. I'd take my chances.

Ace, Pierce, and Tommo were lying across a sofa each watching a movie on the large television screen. For once they didn't have bags of crisps spilling out on their laps. Looked like Snow truly had filled our wolf bellies.

"Anything?" Ace asked as I walked past.

"Not tonight."

"Interesting that since we captured Snow there's been no further action," Tommo noted.

"It's not unusual for a couple of days to go by without another body part in a box, but yes, that had crossed my mind," I replied. I liked that Tommo had the ability to keep a cool head at all times and to stand back from situations and see all viewpoints.

"I don't believe she's involved," he added. "But I had to mention it, just in case."

"It'll be interesting to see what she says about all the evidence tomorrow," Pierce added. "Whether she can uncover a clue."

"I hope so," I answered. "But I'm not holding my breath."

"This has nearly finished and then we're going to watch the Grand Prix," Tommo stated. "You joining us?"

"Yeah. Grab us a beer, will you? I'm just going to get changed and check on Snow. You heard anything from her?"

"She's been in the room since dinner. We asked her if she wanted to join us, but she hasn't. I'm surprised, considering she's stayed to get to know us better," Pierce noted.

"Snow was going to phone her family to explain where she's been. Maybe she's not managed to get away yet? I'll extend the invite again. Dawn will break in a couple more hours and then she'll have lost the opportunity."

It did strike me as strange that she'd stayed in the room.

When I entered my suite and found Snow with red-rimmed eyes, I realised why she'd not gone downstairs.

"What's wrong?" I asked, sitting beside her on the bed. She was sitting up, leaning against the headboard.

"I'm just confused, that's all. I spoke with my father, and he doesn't like me staying here, but said

I'm an adult and it's up to me. He wants you to call him."

"Fair enough."

"But my mum was ready to come and drag me out of here and take me home. She started tearing up and it got to me. Made me feel bad. I don't want to cause my family any hurt, but how do I live my own life, Kellan? How will they feel, especially my mum, if she discovers my meet ups with Andre? It will break her heart if I were to move far away. She lost her own mother after her parents' savage divorce and then her mum died. But I need to feel free, Kellan. It burns inside me."

I squeezed her shoulder, startling a little at the cold flesh that I'd forgotten vampires had. "This is the first time you've left your home properly, Snow, and you got kidnapped by wolves. I think you can cut your mother a little slack on this occasion. She'll get used to you becoming independent, but you're her firstborn. I'm afraid you're treading the path your siblings will follow without as much anguish."

Turning towards the window, I lost myself in the past for a moment. Remembering how my mother used to look at me and fuss. Where most wolves had multiple cubs, my mother had only had me.

"Anyway, enough of my self pity. Did you come across anything useful tonight?" she asked me.

"No." I let out a deep exhale. "The fact we can get no further on, unless we somehow trap this person is of deep frustration to me."

"I'm sorry you're having to go through this. Did your father have enemies that had contact with vampires?"

I rubbed at my forehead. "I was never aware of a single person who didn't like or love my father. We were a peaceful pack. Kept largely to ourselves. Wolves from other packs come to join us because of our reputation. It's a complete mystery, but they'll slip up. And when they do, I'll make sure they pay." I got up from the bed. "I'm just going to have a quick wash and get changed in the bathroom, and then I'm going downstairs to sit with the others. You coming?"

"Yeah, sounds good," she said, watching me as I opened my wardrobe and took out fresh jeans and a t-shirt.

I felt different again when I came out of the bathroom. Just a simple splash of some water on my face and getting out of the dark leathers I'd worn in the woods had me refreshed and more alert.

"Come on then," I gestured to Snow.

"Aren't you forgetting something?" she said, climbing from the bed and waving her phone in front of me.

"I have to do this now?" I protested.

"Right now, or my parents will be here before dawn."

I sighed. "Call them."

"Hey, Dad. I have Kellan here for you to speak to," Snow stated, and then she passed me the phone.

"Why don't you go downstairs, Snow, and watch the Grand Prix with the others. I'll be there shortly," I said.

"I'm guessing that's an order rather than a suggestion," she replied, but a minute later the door closed behind her.

Leaving me to talk with her father.

"Kellan Luna here. I believe I'm speaking to Mr Salinger?" I said in my most polite tone.

"Yes, Beau Salinger. As you can imagine, the fact that you kidnapped my daughter, and she now willingly wishes to stay with you has my interest peaked somewhat. She says you treated her well and then told her she could go. Is that correct?"

"I think I could have treated her better, in all honesty. I let her go hungry, and the fact one of my wolves stabbed her with a stake in order to question her wasn't a great show of my protection. I'm new to all this, Mr Salinger. Did Snow explain about the murder of my father?"

"She told me you'd only been the alpha a month. However, she failed to tell me that someone had stabbed her. Funny that, given she wants to stay with the pack, isn't it?"

"Oh dear. She left out that part?"

"I think I'd better hear things from your point of view so that I have a clear understanding of the truth."

After detailing the facts of Snow's capture and my father's body parts being delivered to me in boxes, I was surprised when Beau began giving me suggestions.

"Measure the boxes. It's more than likely they are widely available, but you never know if it could be a bespoke size, in which case an internet search might reveal the store they've been bought from. Red ribbon is easily accessible. I should know, Snow has plenty of it. I understand why on finding some in her possession and her being a vampire that you suspected she was involved. Also, you're saying it's a vampire due to the lack of blood, but what if that's just been done to get you to think that way? You need to take a step back and review everything anew. It's a good idea to have Snow look through the evidence. It'll give you a fresh perspective."

"I'm very grateful to you for this and for the fact you're not here attempting to drain me for having captured your daughter."

"Part of me wants to, don't think otherwise. But you have been nothing but fair since you captured her. Many alpha wolves would have tortured a vampire found on their patch."

"That's not how my father brought me up. Even with the highest of suspicion, unless we have proof, we do not subject anyone to harm. That's why Nala's actions have brought me anguish."

"I also feel anguish. I feel responsible for Snow's experience as I'm the one who encouraged her to leave the house. She must have had such a fright."

"Now I feel guilty," I said.

"You'll have big choices to make, Kellan, as alpha. I used to deal with a pack when I sold antiques, and there was always something happening. Stealing, drugs, challenges for the role of alpha—"

I interrupted. "—there's none of that here. We're one large happy family."

"Then you're a rarity, because wolves like a fight and sometimes that playfighting becomes something else."

"Would you like me to send Snow home? I can arrange transport for her to ensure she arrives safely," I asked.

"No. My daughter wishes to stay with you for a couple of days. She's an adult. If it's okay with you, then no matter my thoughts on the subject, she can stay. But harm a hair on her head, Kellan, and I'll there to deal with you. Be warned, I don't hide behind box deliveries. I'd deal with you in front of your entire pack and take out anyone else involved while I was at it."

"Received and understood. Our hospitality is extended to your daughter as a guest of the Luna pack. She will be chaperoned at all times to ensure she's kept safe."

"That's all I can ask. Thank you, Kellan. Could I ask you one last favour?"

"Of course."

"Should she begin a relationship with any pack member, would you just ensure she's happy? That's all a father wants for their daughter really."

I almost choked on my own saliva. "Surely you want her to find a vampire mate? Relationships between wolf and vampire are usually frowned upon as it disrupts the usual practices of our species."

"Snow can love whomever she wishes to love as long as they love her so deeply, they'd be willing to die for her. Anyway, right now I'm concerned she might just use her freedom from her family to have a little fun. All I ask is you make sure she's not being taken advantage of."

"You have my word, Beau," I promised.

"Then my daughter can stay," he replied. "I'm back Friday, Kellan, but if you need me before then, either for Snow or if you want my help with your current situation, just call."

"Why would you want to help me?" I asked, genuinely surprised by his offer.

"Because once upon a time I felt desolate about my life. I let my house go to ruin, and largely withdrew from existing. I hear the old me in your voice. Times will change and come good again, Kellan. Keep that fact close in your mind."

"Thank you," I said, before ending the call.

The vampire's gesture was the slow turning on of my sorrow's tap. At first, as the drip hit my hand, I looked at it in astonishment. Then more joined until a torrent of tears poured out of me, my body shuddering, as everything flooded me all at once. I sank to my knees on my pile of blankets and curled up in a foetal position, unable to do anything more.

Chapter 15

Snow

"Snow! We thought you weren't coming," Ace said, sitting up on the sofa to make room for me. He patted his side at the same time as Pierce did the same thing. Tommo remained laid across his sofa, so I walked over to him and made him move up.

"See, guys. Play hard to get, always," Tommo scoffed at the other two.

"I'm not choosing my favourite wolf. This has the best view of the television," I pointed out, settling back to watch the race. I ought to be supporting the UK drivers, but I had a secret crush on Carlos Sainz, so checked the board to see what position he was in.

"What's Kellan doing? He said he was going to invite you to join us and now he's not returned," Ace asked.

"He was talking to my father."

Tommo raised a brow. "Has the shit hit the fan?"

"My dad just wanted to make sure it was okay for me to stay here."

"Yeah, I bet he has nothing to say about the fact we kidnapped you *at all*."

"You're very sarcastic," I noted.

"You're very naïve," he shot back.

"Where's Raina tonight?" I asked him.

"Babysitting her younger brothers and sisters. So there's a space in my bed if you want it."

Ace drew a sharp intake of breath.

"I don't, but thanks. For a start I should imagine your sheets have more jizz than an IVF clinic."

Pierce cackled.

"They probably do," Tommo agreed. "I like you, Snow. You have sass. If you want to clean my bedsheets tomorrow feel free."

"What, so I can climb in your bed afterwards?"

"Only if you can't help yourself," he said.

Then a crash in the race distracted us from teasing each other. Hamilton having been forced out.

I stayed awhile, all of us caught up in the race, with only the odd comment about what we were watching. But after forty-five minutes, I became concerned that

Kellan hadn't returned. Was he *still* chatting with my father?

"I'm going to make my way back upstairs now. Kellan's either still on my phone to my father, or maybe asleep? I'll go check what's happening anyway. Pierce, shall I meet you about four pm tomorrow to go through what evidence you have so far?"

"Sounds like a plan. I'll bring everything here."

"Will you be cooking for us all again tomorrow, Snow?" Tommo asked.

"I'd like to if it's okay with you?"

All three of them nodded.

"And if we wash our own sheets, would you do a quick vampire vacuum around our rooms?" Tommo added.

I laughed. "If you'd like your room cleaning, then please remove anything I might find disagreeable, and I'll see what I can do. Stick a note on the door that it's okay for me to clean up and let the others know please."

"I thought women wanted to share chores these days?" Ace asked.

"I've not volunteered to be your servant. It's about choice, Ace. Right now, I don't mind helping to get your place shipshape. My vampire speed has me at an advantage. But once your rooms are clean then you have a fresh start and should stop being such utter dirty pigs."

"We're dirty wolves, and most women don't complain," Tommo said with a wink.

"Night all," I said. "I'm off upstairs."

"Sweet dreams, Snow," Pierce said. The other two began mimicking him. I left them to it.

I walked into the room, closed the door, and then let out a yelp. There was an enormous wolf laid on its side in front of the bed. Kellan's russet form was still, and I wondered if he was asleep. Until he slowly began to sit up, looking at me.

With half a mind to immediately leave, I took a few steps back towards the door, but Kellan raised a huge paw, yet managed to gently pat the floor in front of him.

He was telling me to approach.

I did so, and the wolf's eyes met mine. He was twice my size and I swallowed nervously. *What would his fur feel like,* I wondered. Picking up my hand and holding it out to the wolf, he sniffed my fingers and then slightly nuzzled them. Feeling brave, I stroked the side of his face, and the underside of his chin, and then I moved to stroke my hands down the fur of his back.

"You are beautiful in wolf form, Kellan," I said. "But could you turn back so I can ask you about the conversation with my father?"

A ripple appeared over him and then Kellan was back to his manly form and once again naked. I threw him an abandoned bath towel from the floor. Smirking, he wrapped it around his head.

"That's not where it's for," I said, snippily.

Kellan slowly removed it and wrapped it around his waist. However, not only had I seen his enormous cock again, but the fact remained that his highly defined abs, biceps, and triceps had me overwhelmed and made my pussy pulse.

"It's okay to not like me, yet be attracted to me," he stated, matter of fact. "As a wolf we are known for our looks, and with my power as the alpha it's just such an aphrodisiac for a woman," he teased.

"Shut up," I told him. I sat down on the edge of the bed. "How was your chat with my father?"

"It went fine actually. Nice chap, your dad."

"Say that again." I couldn't believe my ears.

"I think he appreciated my honesty, and he even gave me some advice with finding our enemy."

"Did he say I can stay?"

"He did. He just asked that I keep an eye on you if you decide to get frisky with the wolves."

My face burned. "I wish I thought you were joking, but given he said something very similar to me himself, I know you're not." I sighed.

"At least he's letting you stay. I'm not sure I'd let any daughter of mine stay in a vampire's nest."

"You can't stop them if they're an adult," I pointed out.

"The hell I can't," he said, giving an indication of what an overprotective father he'd be when he finally had a family.

I just shook my head.

"Why didn't you come down to join everyone else after you'd finished speaking to him?" I asked, changing the subject.

"Just needed a little time alone. You don't get much when you're an alpha." His statement reeked of bullshit and the fact he couldn't meet my eyes confirmed it.

"It's okay to experience emotions other than anger, Kellan. They won't kill you."

"They could kill others if I'm too immersed in myself."

"You're allowed a life. Your father had one. He loved your mother, they had you, and he loved Nala too. You can't shut down your emotions; the future of your pack relies on them. Do you think you'll not love and care for your wife and children? Do you think hardening yourself off will benefit your pack? You lost your father, but they lost their alpha. They'll not grieve openly in front of you if they believe you can't handle it."

He was still looking downward and not meeting my gaze.

"What were you like at the funeral?" I pushed. His shoulders tightened. "Oh." I stopped suddenly, as a thought came to me. "How did you have a ceremony bearing in mind you've not got his body?"

"I vowed not to bury my father until I had all of him."

"No, no, no," I argued. "You must at least have a ceremony, a memorial, even if you wait to bury him. You all need to mourn. For heaven's sake, Kellan."

"I can't face it," he admitted, and that's when I saw the tears welling at the bottom of his eyes.

Moving closer to him and sitting beside him on the blankets was when I noticed his eyes were a little puffy.

"That's why you didn't come downstairs. You were grieving," I exclaimed, reaching out to hug him towards me.

Kellan didn't fight me. Instead, he wept. His head

rested above my chest. His tears soaked through my dress. "That's it, Kellan, let it out," I said.

A minute or so later, he lifted his head and wiped a hand across his face. "Please tell no one of this moment."

"Of course I won't. This is your private business."

He looked at me with a furrowed brow. "I don't know what it is about you, Snow. You manage to reach parts of me others cannot. It's like you were sent to torment me."

"I thought I was helping. How am I tormenting you?" I bit my lip. His eyes moved to my mouth, and then to my chest.

I noticed his heavy breathing and I dropped my gaze to where he was staring. His tears had made the top of my white dress transparent where my right breast was, and my rosy areole could be seen clearly.

"How are you tormenting me? By being but a hair's breadth away from me, and yet impossible for me to touch." His voice was low and husky.

I gasped. The tension between us had built so much I felt I'd be able to grasp it with my hand. Like elastic about to snap.

"What if I said you *can* touch me?" I whispered.

"You're not a wolf," he said.

"I'm not proposing marriage," I shot back. "Just touch me, for fuck's sake."

His patience snapped, and his mouth came upon mine in a claiming. He pushed me onto my back and devoured my lips in the most exquisite kiss I'd ever received in my life.

But as quick as he'd dived on me, he retreated.

"Go to bed, Snow," he barked out, as if I was making him sick.

"Wh-what's wrong?"

"You may not be part of the vendetta against my father, Snow, but you also threaten my very sanity, and I can't afford this distraction right now. I'm going to turn back into my wolf and sleep now. I bid you goodnight."

"Well, I don't regret what happened. I do regret that you stopped though." I huffed.

His eyes narrowed. "It's been but an hour or so since I promised your father I'd keep you safe. Fucking you when there's no future to it is not something I'm going to do. I sleep with people outside of here where I leave no trace. It's better that way." His face began to take on that uncaring mask he wore when he shut down.

"I appreciate your honesty," I said. "Goodnight, Kellan."

He nodded. "I know I allowed you to pet me before, but I'd be grateful if you'd leave me be now. I just thought you'd be interested in how a wolf felt. There was nothing more to it."

"Message received and understood." Getting to my feet, I walked away from him and climbed under the duvet, grabbing my backpack on my way. As Kellan changed to his wolf-like form and laid down among his blankets, closing his eyes, I took out the secret journal and pen my brother had gifted me. Opening it, I began to write.

I am currently living amongst seven wolves in a cabin. Who would have believed this only a few days ago when I was given this journal. My gratitude to my brother for the idea and for the fact it carries a lock so I may unburden myself of my thoughts and feelings with no recourse.

Tonight, Kellan kissed me. I burned with the passion of it and now I am back feeling like there is something within me that needs to be quenched. All of the wolves are so beautiful and knowing that they sometimes share a woman led me to making myself come tonight. What is happening to me? Tomorrow night, I MUST run with the wolves, as I don't feel cooking and cleaning will do anything to remove this ache in me. I want to feel satisfied, and right now, I'm holding myself back from going out of the room, out of the cabin, and throwing myself out of trees in order to break my bones to feel the wrongness of it all and then the welcome discomfort as everything knits back together.

Dawn is beginning to break and I am grateful for the exhaustion now slowly seeping through me. I can only hope I wake up feeling rested and not restless.

I quickly undressed and put on my pyjamas. After locking the journal, I wrapped it within my white dress and placed it at the bottom of my backpack.

With one last look at Kellan's now sleeping form, I sank further down my bed and fell asleep.

Chapter 16

Kellan

Usually, I couldn't sleep when my mind was tormented. But on this occasion my body was happy to shut down in order to block out reality. I slept for five hours, finally waking just after eight am.

After turning back into my human form, I stood and stretched, deciding after a quick breakfast I would go to the gym for a short workout before making my way to the office. I felt bent out of shape and the reason why slept in my bed.

I walked slowly over to Snow's sleeping form. She looked so peaceful, and I smiled at her pink pyjamas. They were adorned with cartoon black bats with cute smiley faces. The woman had caught me in a vulnerable state last night, and that was something no one should ever find me in. I couldn't afford that loss of control.

With a renewed sense of purpose, I quickly dressed, and went downstairs, pleased to discover there was no one around. I fixed myself a quick omelette and a coffee, then grabbed my gym stuff and set off. I'd shower there after I'd worked off this inner feeling of guilt.

I allowed myself the luxury of a slow stroll there, giving my food a chance to digest a little and also ensuring I said good morning and chatted to as many of my pack as were around. It was around thirty minutes later I finally reached the gym, quickly changing into my kit and heading for the treadmill first.

Nothing beat a run in the woods and tonight we'd agreed to do so, and to allow Snow to join us.

Snow.

Not two minutes into my routine and she was on my mind again. The quicker she left here the better.

My mind recollected the feel of my lips on hers and the hunger within me that urged me to claim her. That weird feeling had returned to the pit of my stomach, the one like a furled snake waiting to be tempted from its basket. Snow the song that could encourage it.

It couldn't happen. An alpha with an enemy

needed to concentrate on that. And then I would look for a mate. It was time. I needed to show the pack that we had longevity, by my breeding the next generation, including the next alpha-to-be.

For some reason I thought then of Nala's crystal ball. Despite my previous non-belief, I found myself wondering who the ball had shown as my mate. When I spoke with Nala later, I would discuss my plans and see if she came forth with any vision she'd seen. It was possible she'd asked it again since then, given its warning.

"Seriously, are you really now beginning to believe in that hogwash," I mumbled quietly to myself.

"Alpha Kellan, is your grumbling to yourself and trying to outrun the treadmill an indication of an inner frustration?" Aspen, one of the gym trainers, asked. While I answered, I began appraising her potential suitability as the mother of my children. How could I know she could carry cubs? Did I have to request my future mate be checked out physically? Did I have to wait for the mate bond first and would that know what it was looking for? Or would the mate bond come later? My father had immediately felt the bond with my mother but had dated Nala for a time before it had pinged for him a second time.

Why did everything have to be so complicated?

"Okay, Kellan. With how you're currently grinding your teeth, may I suggest you climb off the treadmill and come with me to the punch bags," Aspen stated. It wasn't so much a suggestion as an order.

Switching the treadmill off, I followed her through to the boxing section.

Aspen helped me wrap my hands and then gave me a pair of gloves. We walked over to the bag and she started me off with some warm ups, and then training. It helped ease some of the frustration within me.

"Now punch the ever-loving shit out of it, Kellan, because I'd rather you risked an injury on this, than lost it with one of the pack," she said. I paused and turned to her.

"Is it that obvious?"

"Maybe not to other people, but I'm trained to see how people hold themselves and I learn what they've come to the gym to do. You've walked in this morning like an unexploded bomb. I know you've much to deal with after your father's death and we know you currently have a vampire staying with you…"

"Times are truly testing right now," I admitted. "The vampire is fine. She's just staying a couple of days to see how wolves live. Allowing her to stay was the least I could do given that we'd kept her prisoner."

"Are we going to get to meet her soon then?" Aspen queried.

"She wants to come on a run tonight, so anyone coming tonight will meet her there."

"That's good. We're not used to a vampire among us. Some of us have felt a little uncomfortable about it." She fiddled with a lock of her chestnut hair.

"I appreciate you saying that to me. My mind has been so full of protecting you all, that I've forgotten to discuss things with you all."

Another wolf wandered over to Aspen. "Hey, Asp, I'm here."

"Personal training client," Aspen explained. "If you go insane on that bag, make sure to ice your hands afterwards."

"Actually, I'm feeling much better after our chat." It was the truth. I thought of what Beau had said to me about sometimes needing to take a step back and look at things anew. I'd do that today. I'd make a point to converse with people and listen to what they had to say. To include my pack. The run tonight would be a great bonding experience and then I'd invite everyone to the bar for a few beers and a dance.

I said my goodbyes and went for my shower.

I thought Nala might be in a subdued mood when I saw her, but she actually had her office door open and walked out as I walked into the office block.

"I'm ready to talk when you are," she informed me, her shoulders back and her chin up. There was a visible tautness in her neck.

"No time like the present," I said. "Where do you want to do this?"

"I'll come to your office. Give me two minutes to grab a glass of water."

Nodding my head, I walked into my own office, switching on my laptop and getting comfortable.

Not long after, Nala walked in and sat down on the chair opposite. She sat stiffly with her hands folded, clearly eager to get this conversation out of the way.

"Do you still maintain that you weren't trying to murder the vampire?" I pressed.

"Absolutely. As I said before, I was trying to find out if she was involved quicker, instead of with all the politically correct taking forever nonsense I felt you were doing." She held up a hand at my opened mouth. "I know now I was in the wrong. Not only because it wasn't my place, but also as I realised it wasn't how your father would have dealt with it either. I allowed my grief and frustration to take the lead on my decision making. I am very sorry, Kellan. As alpha you know there is a way to proceed. As a grieving widow, I made a large error in judgement which could have led to Snow's death if she'd have moved while I staked her."

The conversation I'd envisaged having with Nala this morning wasn't going to happen after Aspen had reminded me about the pack's wanting knowledge, and Beau's advice to step back. In front of me I now saw my father's grieving widow, instead of an annoying female wolf who kept forgetting her place.

"It must be very difficult for you, Nala. Having lost your husband, and that leading to a different role within the pack too," I said gently.

"I didn't get to say goodbye. That morning, he left early to go for a run, and he never came back." She stared into space. "Most mornings I stirred when he got ready because the clumsy oaf usually dropped something on the floor, but that night I'd complained and made him get everything ready beforehand. Santos did so. Then climbed into bed and snuggled me close. All I can think about is how much he showed he loved me, and my last words to him had been me complaining."

"Oh, Nala. He knew how much you loved him. Dad told me often about how he'd never thought he'd meet anyone else after my mother. He adored you." I decided to be truthful. "And I'm sorry because I held resentment towards you for that. I didn't like the fact someone had, to me, taken my mother's place at my father's side."

"I know. I understood that. But I couldn't help the fact I'd fallen in love with your dad and that we bonded. If I'd been able to walk away, I would have, knowing how it made you feel having to share your father's time with me."

And that's when I saw the deep-seated sorrow Nala had previously kept from me. It wasn't just that she was grieving my father. It wasn't that she'd kept me at a distance because she didn't want to encourage me to share her time with my father. It was because she couldn't avoid loving my father, but she could try to avoid loving me.

"This is because of your son, isn't it? That's why you kept me at a distance."

"I didn't want to risk loving another child. Losing another wasn't something I could stand. The fact you resented me made it easier to stay back. It's why I didn't give your father any cubs. Not because I couldn't as everyone assumed, but due to the fact I mentally could not go through it. Also, I didn't think you'd have been impressed by stepsiblings making you share your time with your father further. No, it was easier for me to keep my distance from you and let you think whatever you wanted about me. But now your father is no longer here, and I see it written in your face how much you want me to leave."

My breath hitched.

"I will go as soon as we find your father's killer. Even though this is my home. I've started afresh before, and I'll do it again."

"No, Nala. Your home is here. I've been an arrogant fool with my head up my arse. Do you know the irony of what's made me see the truth? It was Snow's father of all people. I've hated all vampires. Wanted to destroy them all given my father's death, and yet it took a conversation with Beau last night and then a chat with Aspen at the gym this morning, to make me realise I've been so consumed by the loss of my father that I've not thought of anyone else."

"That's not true. You put the pack before yourself."

"But I don't consider their feelings. I just follow protocol."

I shook my head in wonder at how I'd been so wrapped up in my need to do things by the book and with my desire for vengeance.

"It's like I just woke up today, Nala, from some obsessed state. What you did to Snow was wrong, but I understand where it came from. There will be no punishment from me. I actually wish I could alleviate your suffering from grief and loss. I can't bring back my father, but is there any way to make contact with your son?"

"He could be anywhere. Though I thought it best at first not to look for him, after a year or so I couldn't help myself. I missed him so much. But I found no trace and as the years passed, I thought that maybe too much time had gone by. That it was too late."

"It's never too late, Nala. What if he's looking for you too?"

"I wouldn't really know where to start now. Anyway, you *can* bring back your father, by finding the rest of his body."

"We could ask Snow about your son?" I said, ignoring her comment about my dad. "There must be a way of searching for other vampires, like we know the other wolf packs."

That amused Nala who sniggered. "Yes, I'm sure Snow will be delighted to help the woman who almost dusted her."

"Leave it with me," I said.

We both fell silent.

"I will do everything I can to find the rest of my

father, but in the meantime, perhaps it's time for us to think of holding a memorial."

"Really? I think that would help the pack enormously at this time of uncertainty while this enemy is still at large."

"Would you help me organise it, Nala?"

"I'd be honoured. Kellan, please apologise to Snow on my behalf. I know she won't want to see me. I wouldn't want to see me either. But let her know I am truly sorry."

"I will. Now, there is something else, and I don't want you to laugh when I ask."

"Oh?"

"Your crystal ball thing. I was passing your office and I heard it say something about a new alpha's mate. Did it show you anything?"

"Yes," she replied. "It showed me Snow."

Chapter 17

SNOW

Of course, the first thing I did on waking was to see if Kellan was there. Finding the room empty, the second thing I did was to feel in my backpack for my journal. That was thankfully still there also, though if Kellan decided to go through my belongings and read it, that would be his problem when he came across my true feelings. I wasn't ashamed of my attraction to the wolves.

I made the most of having the room to myself and enjoyed a leisurely bath, and then noting it was almost four pm, I dried my hair and put my white dress back on. If I was going to be doing chores shortly, I may as well re-wear this day-old dress. I missed not having my ribbon in my hair, but instead took out a cream scrunchie I'd thrown in from Gene's present and tied my hair back with that.

Then I left the room.

"Pierce is in the dining room," Trent told me, as he looked up from the sofa.

"I need my breakfast first," I said, rubbing my tummy.

"I take it you mean your blood from the fridge, although I'm sure Pierce would be willing to be a snack. He's in the dining room after all."

"Ha ha. Did the others tell you I'd offered to clean your rooms?"

"My door is wide open for you, also for if you want to clean."

I playfully swatted his hair. "You going for the run tonight?"

"Wouldn't miss it. We're not long off the full moon now and our need to run is ramping up."

"What happens at the full moon then?" I queried. "Because you can change to wolf form at any time."

"Choice is taken away at the full moon. We all become wolf whether we want to or not. It's also when mating rituals take place. If anyone wants to make it official, it's done on the full moon. Mate-bonded shifters will fuck as wolves and bite each other's necks. Then they'll screw again in human form."

"Ahhh, I see."

"Whereas tonight we can fuck without consequence."

"I get it."

"Just wanted to make that very clear." His gaze lingered on mine.

"I'm looking forward to joining the wolves tonight," I said. Then I gave him a teasing wink and turned in the direction of the kitchen.

I'd decided to rule nothing out, but I kept my focus on going for the run and observing the pack.

Feeling replenished after my blood, I went next door and found Pierce sorting things into piles. My eyes rested on the four black boxes, their red ribbons in front.

"Hey," I said.

"Sleep well?" he enquired.

"Like the dead," I joked, getting a laugh in response from Pierce.

"Here's everything," he said, gesturing around. "The boxes with their contents. They've been brought from the cold store we've kept them in, but as you can imagine, the fact they're now in a warm room…"

"I have a superior sense of smell, so let me look at these quickly and then you can get them out of here."

Pierce nodded.

I walked around and removed the lid from the first box, recoiling as I saw Santos' head. Not because it was unexpected, but because even in death, I could see the resemblance to his son. "Could have warned me he looked like Kellan," I said tersely.

"Shit, I never thought. We're just used to that." Pierce stretched his lips in an apologetic grimace.

"Sorry, it just took me by surprise a little. I'm sure you had the same response when the box first arrived. Tell me about how it was delivered."

"A driver who was bringing a large food delivery, asked for Kellan, and said he'd found a box in his van addressed to him."

"And the driver had no idea where he'd got the box from?"

"No."

"Could you to try to find the details of the drivers if you can? Or the date and time of delivery. There would be a delivery note, right?"

"Yes. We kept it. It's in that pile there."

My eyes followed his pointing finger.

"That's good. Because if I can get to the driver, I can use compulsion to check he really was innocent."

"Of course. That would be fantastic," Pierce said.

"Anyway, back to this." I looked back in the box. The smell of death was unmistakeable, but I smelled nothing else, other than the scent of Pierce, and a low trace of the other wolves' smells including Nala's.

I held my lips with my right fingers, pondering. "Had there been any argument between Santos and Nala prior to this?"

"You think Nala did it?" Pierce's eyes almost bugged out of his head.

"I'm looking at all angles. There is no scent of anyone outside the pack."

"That's because they've disguised it."

"Who says? That's something you've surmised, but what if it's Nala? What if she's made it look like a vampire did it. She was married to one, wasn't she? Which means she'd know exactly what to do."

"Fuck."

"I'm not saying she has done it." I held up my palms. "But I'm here to observe and note things and the fact she staked me yesterday morning doesn't help."

I opened the next box and found Santos' tongue. "If you killed someone after an argument, you might cut out their tongue in spite, might you? It's what we use to speak after all." I frowned.

"The same note came with the first few boxes. Shall we read it before you finish looking at the boxes?" Pierce suggested.

"Good idea." I waited while he passed me the note.

I cast my eyes over the words and Pierce stood by my side reading over my shoulder.

Piece by piece
 I'll return him to you
 The ruination of my life
 Your only clue
 I abide by the words:
 Do unto others
 As they have done to you.

"Santos didn't ruin Nala's life though, did he? He made her happy. So unless there's something about their relationship we're not privy too, it's unlikely. I'll talk to Kellan later and see if there was anything that happened between them at the time of Santos going missing."

I passed the note back and looked in the next box at the hand, and then the final one: the heart. Then I returned to the head, lifting it.

"All have been drained, but I see no puncture wounds in the neck. If they'd been kind enough to send the wrists attached to the hands, I could have checked those too. If it was a vampire, I'm guessing they drained from the wrist, and that could be why they haven't sent them," I surmised.

"See, you're giving us new details and possibilities already," Pierce said.

"Can you pass me the last note that's been received so far?"

"Just a sec." A moment later I was reading it.

A tongue returned
   But unable to form words
   Mine still present
   But never observed
   My life ruined piece by piece
   I'll do unto others
   As they have done to me.

"So the tongue was the final item delivered, and that's what was found beside me?" I double checked.

Pierce nodded.

"So the person who's doing this is someone with a

definite vendetta against either Santos, Kellan, or another member of the pack." I sat down and Pierce sat beside me with an iPad in his hand. "They feel they've never had a voice, so there's a grudge there that they've not been noticed or listened to. And this has ruined their life, slowly, as they say piece by piece. So that would suggest this grudge has formed over time."

"Go on," Pierce encouraged.

"If their target was simply Santos, then killing him would have been the end of it. Why send body parts in separate boxes if you've dealt with your enemy? Wouldn't you just kill and be done, thankful to get away with it?"

"Whereas if you've still got a vendetta, you'd continue to send them." Pierce warmed to my way of thinking. "Which leaves it being against Kellan or the pack in general."

"Yes, which puts you all in danger."

"I'm noting down all your thoughts, so we can review it as a pack later."

"And that's the final possibility," I said.

"What is?"

"That it's one of the pack. It could even be one of the council."

Pierce shook his head passionately. "Absolutely not. We'd never do that."

"As I said, I'm just laying it all out there. It's a shame you all have the mind guard that doesn't let me read you. I could have listened in tonight at the run, or you could have come for a walk with me around the compound. I might have uncovered something."

"Oh, one other thing," Pierce said. "Kellan told me that your father had suggested checking if the boxes themselves were a clue. I did, but they're a generic brand you can get from anywhere."

"I wouldn't expect a killer to be that stupid that they'd pick a bespoke box that led us straight to them," I said. I got up and picked up the ribbons. "These are just generic ribbons. I can tell you that because I purchase similar myself. That's all I've got, Pierce. I hope it helps."

"I'm sure it will. Thank you, Snow. I need to relay this to Kellan and then take it from there. I'll go put everything back away, and then spend some time having a mull over the things you've mentioned."

"I'm going to go clean the rooms, and then make tonight's meal. I'll see you at dinner."

"You will indeed. Thank you again, Snow," he said, giving me that smile that held within it the invite for more.

"Anytime," I said, hoping he understood that I was open to possibilities.

The wolves' rooms weren't as bad as I thought they'd be. Possibly they'd tidied before I went in, like some people did before a cleaner came around. I did a quick dust and vacuum. The rest of keeping it tidy was their responsibility.

After that, I took up residence in the kitchen and decided to make a spaghetti Bolognese with an enormous amount of mince. Then I made rum and caramel bananas for dessert. I wasn't sure if bananas and pasta benefitted wolves in the same way they did humans when they ran or worked out, but I figured it couldn't hurt.

The thought made me laugh at myself. I looked like a human, but I didn't need pasta or bananas to whizz around, did I? God, I was an idiot. The food smelled delicious anyway, but it showed I did need to learn more about wolf shifters and their diets.

With everything prepared, I decided to go change into one of my other two clean outfits. I pulled out my blue dress with its laced bodice and lemon skirt. The red lace that laced up the bodice gave me pause, so I looked around and found some shoes of Kellan's. The huge shoes thankfully had huge laces. I rethreaded the bodice with a large black shoelace and put the red lace into my backpack. Then I let my hair out of its bun, and it fell in soft waves having been scrunched up.

That was better. I looked and felt much more myself in my favourite dress. Walking out of the room, I walked straight into Kellan's solid chest.

"Ooomph," I said, while taking a deep satisfying inhale of wolf pheromones.

Chapter 18

Kellan

"Did you just sniff me?" I asked the woman whose face was still snuffled into my chest.

She backed out but couldn't move far as the door was behind her. As she lifted her head, I took a step back.

"Sue me. You smell nice, and I have an excellent sense of smell."

I was trying not to think about the crystal ball's prediction, having rolled my eyes at Nala, and declared it hogwash. Snow was pitching me ever closer to insanity with her proximity, but I couldn't help but smile. I don't think she realised just how amusing some of her statements were, even if they were a fact.

"I'm just off to finish the dinner. I'll shout when it's ready."

"You really don't have to do this you know. No one will want you to leave."

She laughed. "I'll stay no later than Friday. I want to be home when my family return. I may even go home tomorrow to enjoy one day of being alone in the house. I'll consider things when I've done the run and met some more of the pack."

"Whatever works for you."

"Do you think I could come back and visit sometime?" she asked.

"I don't think that's a good idea," I replied. "Especially while our pack is under threat. I think it's best you try to find your place with your own kind. There must be someone you can talk to about how you're feeling. Some kind of elder."

Snow scoffed. "Don't worry about it. That's for me to sort out. There's no wonder wolves and vampires become sworn enemies when words like 'your kind' get used. I thought we were all individuals, but no, I'm just a bloodsucker and better go find some other bats to hang upside down with." She pushed past me and down the stairs, and I listened as kitchen equipment was banged around.

The truth was I wanted her to leave so we could get back to focusing on my father's murder. Then when we'd dealt with that, and it *would* happen, I was going to find my mate... my real one, not the image Nala had clearly misinterpreted.

"Dinner's ready," Snow called, and we slowly made our way down to the dining room.

"Wow, you look incredible, Snow," Samuel exclaimed. I looked at my friends and all were in awe of our guest. It was true though. She did look lovely.

We sat down to eat and as she plated up the pasta, we all stared down at our plates.

"Have I done something wrong?" she asked.

"Not at all. It's just we don't have pasta very often. It will make a nice change," Tommo reassured her.

But Snow wasn't having it.

She slumped. "I should have studied you more to see what you ate. I've done pasta and bananas for energy as if you're human, but you're not, you're werewolves."

"But that's adorable," Tommo pouted.

"Shut up." She narrowed her eyes at him. "Ugh."

"Snow, we eat everything. We just have to ensure we get a large amount of meat, and you've done that." I pointed to the pasta sauce.

"There's something missing though," Tommo

postulated. "Oh, I know. Garlic bread. Any reason why not, Snow?"

"You'll be missing your teeth if you don't stop teasing me," Snow yelled.

"Is it true then that you can't have garlic?" Pierce asked.

"Yes. We have a sensitivity to it. Looks like I have a sensitivity to feeling foolish too." Snow sighed. "Sorry for my outburst."

Tommo finished a huge mouthful. "It's delicious, Snow, honestly. You know I'd tell you if it wasn't."

"That's true." She looked around us. "Are you okay with this meal? Really? I could quickly make something else."

"It's lovely. But don't laugh at us as we drip the sauce everywhere because we don't have a lot of practice with getting spaghetti on a fork," Trent told her. "Wrapping women around my finger? Yes, effortless. But wrapping spaghetti on this fork? Work in progress."

Snow laughed at that, and we all breathed a sigh of relief as eating the meal resumed.

It was as we sat back after the delicious bananas with rum that we lost our fight to behave.

Snow was sitting at the table and had been asking us about wolf life. "When you are wolves tonight will you lick each other?" she asked, receiving a stunned silence. Then her cheeks went rosy. "I meant lick, as in grooming each other," she shrieked.

It was too late, seven wolf shifters were clutching their full stomachs, groaning with laughter.

"Oh, shut up," she said.

I half expected Snow to make her excuses about coming out with us then, but she didn't. All our eyes fixed on her in utter astonishment when she walked downstairs in black sparkly leggings, a black cami, and a matching jacket. I don't think she realised she'd rendered us all speechless.

The leggings hugged her arse, and the cami dipped to show her cleavage. I didn't look at any of my roomies' groins, but I was sure their joggers would be tented. The fact most turned towards the door though was evidence enough. I decided to stare at the trainers on her feet instead.

"Okay, Snow. Stay at my pace please. I know you can whizz around a lot faster than any of us wolves, but I want you to concentrate on the slower movement of your thighs and pumping your arms. Let's see if slowing it down gives you the extra component you feel you're missing."

"What's missing?" Pierce asked. "Anything I can help with?"

"Can I have a quick word with you all?" she said. Fuck, she was going to tell them.

They nodded.

"When I'm a vampire I sometimes don't feel like I've worked off enough energy," she said. "I can't put it into words, but I feel something is missing. I'm going to try to run like a wolf as opposed to zipping around like a vampire and see if exercising slower makes any difference."

"There are plenty of ways we wolves work off our extra energy if a run doesn't suffice," Diego teased.

"I've tried fucking and that didn't do it either," Snow declared, making a few of the others gasp.

She rolled her eyes heavenward. "I know my name is Snow, but could you all kindly remember I'm a vampire, and also not a saint," she huffed. "Now are we going to run, or not?"

We moved through the house, and once outside I turned to her. "Stay with me, remember? You know my wolf and he knows you. He'll keep you safe."

"But what if that isn't what I want?" she said, and she began running after the others. Sighing, I followed.

As we kept a jogger's pace, more of the Luna pack began to join us from their own cabins, and soon there were around sixty of us. As we hit the woods, we changed into our wolves. Mine could see Snow as clearly as I could in human form, but I could scent her better and run faster. I pushed myself to pick up the pace, sailing past the others and taking the lead. Being the alpha I was born to be.

Snow easily matched my pace, but she grinned and laughed with sheer joy as the wind flew through her hair. Then she entertained me as she whipped around nearby trees. After running for around an hour, we entered a large treeless area where we always stopped after a run. I ground to a halt and Snow did too. Other wolves joined us and that's where Snow began to learn more of wolf life.

Some wolves began to playfight, and here we treated everyone as equal. Male and female wolves could fight without there being a sexual element to it, and female wolves were not weaker in strength than their male counterparts. Snow stood watching in fascination as wolves began to push and shove each other, knocking each other out of the way and then diving back on each other for another round of fun.

Scratches appeared where claws had been clumsy, but no one minded. It was part of being a wolf. "They're like me," Snow said, and at first, I didn't understand, until I *did*.

She meant they used up their energy fighting, and it was okay if they got hurt. It was just part of the play. She was right and yet when she'd told me about how her and this Andre guy had fought and injured each other I'd had nothing but concern. But this was what she needed. Not the run, not the sex, but the fight.

So I roared, my eyes flashing amber, raised my paw, ensuring my claws were nowhere near her, and I knocked her off her feet. She landed flat on her back and stared up at me in shock.

Then her eyes turned red, her fangs descended, and she flew to her feet. I stood and waited for her next move. Before I could blink, she'd launched at me with her right leg high and kicked me so hard I fell backwards myself. She sat astride me laughing in my face. It appeared I'd severely underestimated Snow's strength.

I could only hope she didn't kick my alpha arse in front of all my pack. But hey, Snow wanted to fight and so we would. I was the safest option for her, and I knew if I didn't take her on, she'd challenge one of the others. No, it was better it was me.

Grabbing Snow by the hips, I lifted her up,

swinging her above my head, and then back again, releasing my grip so she sailed through the air where she narrowly missed a tree trunk. Breaking off a branch, she ran and swung it at me. I skirted it, snatched it from her, and threw it behind me. There would be no risk of accidental stakings here tonight. But Snow was goading me because she wanted more than play. She wanted the pain. After she punched me in the ear, making it ring, I body slammed her into the nearest tree before taking a step back. She stood up, stretching her neck from side to side, and *laughed*.

I didn't even see her next move it was so fast, but she grabbed my scruff and dragged me along the ground for a few feet before I escaped her grasp, swung myself around and grabbed her by the hair. I wrapped it around my claws and tugged, knowing it would pull on her scalp.

"Pull harder," she commanded, and so I did to her what she'd done to me, dragging her along the ground, knowing twigs and branches would be tearing at her top, maybe tearing at her skin. Some wolves had now stopped to watch us. Others didn't give a damn and carried on with their own playfights.

The next thing I knew, Snow kicked me straight in the face. I grabbed her shoulders and launched her at a large boulder. I'd misjudged my throw though and rather than hit it with her stomach, she smacked into it with her face. I'd gone too far. For wolves it didn't matter where we landed, but I didn't want to see Snow's beautiful face damaged. I knew she craved this, but I wasn't sure I could do it.

Reverting back into my human form, I quickly re-dressed.

But then Snow walked back towards me. Her nose cracked as it moved back into place, the broken skin on her cheeks knitted together, and her mangled chin healed over. Her red eyes shone with elation, and she wore the widest smile I'd ever seen on her. She looked like she'd won the lottery.

Now I could plainly see how she needed this, why it caused her such frustration to have to hide the part of herself where she thrived.

Standing there in the aftermath of the fight, she had never looked more beautiful. But it was nothing to do with her outside appearance. It was a glow that shone brightly now from within.

But I still felt unsettled about having caused her harm. Because she wasn't a wolf and she wasn't one of my pack.

Chapter 19

Snow

I felt elated. The run at the wolves' pace had worked my muscles harder, rather than my just allowing the vampire speed to take over. When I'd seen the wolves playfight, I'd been desperate to join in. I couldn't believe that Kellan had seen that and answered my call.

But his face didn't look elated.

He looked full of remorse.

Did he not see this was exactly what I needed?

"Kellan, we need to get something straight here. If you fought a female wolf in this way, would you have guilt?" I accused.

"No, because we would both be wolves," he answered coolly.

"Okay, so is it because I'm a vampire, or because

apart from my eyes and fangs I still look like a human woman that's making you feel bad?"

His expression gave me the answer.

I raised my hands in frustration. "I'm not human, Kellan. I need people to look past that. Plus, women cage fight you know. They fight underground. I'm consenting to this. I'm not some poor woman subject to her husband's cowardly fists."

"I'm aware of that. It's why I chose to playfight with you. But you can't expect my brain to just reroute itself as quickly as that," he argued.

I sighed. "Fair point."

"Anyhow, has that satisfied your urge?" he asked.

I nodded. "I'm happy to watch everyone else for a bit now."

"Good. I'm going to go and mingle with the pack. Why don't you do the same?" He walked away, and I looked around me.

I felt eyes on me and spotted Raina sitting on the ground with two other women. She waved me over.

"Snow, this is Aspen and Annie."

"Hey," I said. They both smiled and seemed welcoming enough.

"We were not expecting you to join in the fight," Annie, a petite, short-haired blonde said.

"Me neither." I smiled. "But it was just what I needed."

"Do vampires do anything like this? Meet up and mingle?" Raina asked.

"Not like this in the open air. Vampires tend to favour more solitary pursuits. But where I live I've only known my family and a few vampires in the area that I saw at school etc. I've not really experienced much of the world," I admitted.

"Ah, I remember Tommo saying now. You'd gone out for the first time on your own when they captured you."

"Yup. Not exactly encouraging me to travel more."

"But why did you stay when they said you could go?" Aspen asked. Her eyes flicked to Kellan and then back to me.

"I know it seems strange," I acknowledged. "This started out as a nightmare for me. But I figured I was here now, so why not learn about wolf shifters? I'm aiming to stay until Friday lunchtime and then I'll go home to my family. I hope that's okay with everyone else in the pack. I'll be out of all your hair soon."

"It's not connected to Kellan then?" Aspen winked. "Only you and him had some amazing chemistry going there. That fight was hot."

"Truth?" I said, and all the women leaned in eagerly.

"Yes?" Raina urged.

"They're all hot. I don't know how you women cope with looking at these hunky men all day. I'd be permanently changing my underwear."

All three bellowed with laughter.

"You get to know them and realise that beyond those good looks, some of them are complete idiots," Aspen commented. "And then with the other ones, if we feel horny and they do, we just fuck."

My eyes widened. "But doesn't that get complicated?"

"We see sex as a natural way to offload tension. We eat, we drink, we play, we have sex. Things change when the mate bond comes, and then all we want is our partner. Everyone else fades into the background once that happens."

"Yeah, so like if you want to fuck Tommo, don't mind I was in his bed the other day. It's just scratching an itch," Raina added. "Tonight, I have my eye on Leto." She pointed to a dark-haired man chatting to other males. He caught her looking and smiled. Yeah, they were fucking later all right, I could feel the frisson in the air from here.

"And if you do sleep with them, it's not an exclusive thing and we might sleep with them after," Annie noted.

"Got it," I replied. I stared at the fighting happening around me, envious of the wolves' freedom to expel energy in such a way.

"Does the playfighting sometimes lead to sex?" I asked.

"More often than not. Some would already be fucking by now, either in wolf form, or back to their human side. However, our alpha has invited us all for drinks. So tonight, first we drink, and then we screw." Raina raised an imaginary glass. "Cheers to that."

The other two women met her cheers with their own imaginary glasses. They looked at me. Laughing, I clinked my own fake glass.

"Cheers," I said.

"Snow!" Diego shouted, approaching us. "Come on, it's time to get merry. Let's make our way to the bar."

And so we did. Some wolves walked naked carrying their clothes. Others—like the three women—had got dressed. The bar was positioned just a little way from the stores and next to a restaurant. The pack had their own little town, rather than having to go into the main ones. Was there such a thing with vampires too? Places where they all lived away from humans.

There must be. There was so much about life I didn't know.

All the wolves waited outside the bar. Kellan walked to the front and pushed open the door, fixing it in place with a hook.

"The drinks are on me, pack," he shouted. "Do your worst, but have the best time doing so!"

The pack cheered and then I was swept up with the crowd and pushed along into the bar.

My heightened senses made the effects of drinking alcohol stronger to me than to others. Therefore, two beers in, I was feeling mellow and amazing. I'd sat chatting to some more of the pack, wolves of all different ages, and was currently sitting with Pierce, Trent, and Tommo's mothers.

"Pierce says you're hoping he settles down soon," I asked his mum, the alcohol loosening my tongue.

"Yes. He's been a wild one has my eldest. If anyone ever took a fight too far, it was Pierce. If anyone was ever caught up to no good... Pierce. He's grown up a lot since becoming one of Kellan's inner circle and moving into the shared house. I think becoming a father could be the making of him."

"I can't imagine him being naughty." I laughed.

"Never underestimate the quiet ones," she said, smiling.

"Trent hides his feelings with humour," his mother said. "I keep telling him he needs to show his true self, but he doesn't listen."

"Do they ever?" Pierce's mum retorted, making us laugh.

"Tommo's a misery guts. Has he offended you yet? I spoiled him as a child, but instead of being grateful, it's made him a lazy man who expects things without effort. I'll have to apologise to anyone he mate bonds with," his mother noted with a weary sigh.

"I've only known them a few days, but they all seem fine to me. I've seen everything you say, but their real personalities shine through it. They're all good guys and one day they'll mate bond and you'll get lots of lovely grandcubs I'm sure," I reassured them.

Trent chose that point to 'whoop' really loudly and whip his top off before jumping on a table and grinding his hips.

"Just maybe not today," I added, and we all laughed again.

Looking around, I'd noticed Nala hadn't attended this evening, and for that I was grateful. Even though I felt a little drunk, my vampire senses were still on high alert in case any of these shifters saw me as an enemy rather than a visitor.

Then Tommo, Pierce, and Trent all began to head in my direction. "That's enough time spent gossiping with our mothers," Trent said. "It's time to dance."

Tommo grabbed my hand and pulled me to my feet.

"Catch you later," I said to their mums.

"She won't," Pierce said, "time for you old ones to go home as the real party is about to begin."

"I told you not to be fooled by him," Pierce's mother reminded me. "I can see the devil himself in him right now."

Pierce laughed. "Want to dance with the devil?" he asked me.

"Hell yeah," I answered.

"Aww, I wanted to say that," Trent complained. "Woman's stealing my jokes."

"Shut up and get to the dance floor for God's sake before there's no room," Tommo moaned.

Doubling over, I clutched my stomach. Their mothers had described their sons perfectly.

I had tears in my eyes I was laughing so hard.

Kellan came to our side. "Make sure she doesn't drink anymore," he ordered, and then he walked off.

"Party pooper. It's not up to him what I do," I harumphed.

"Kind of is while you're here because he's the alpha," Trent pointed out.

"Then let's dance until I sober up," I announced, cheering.

I danced like a drunken dad at a disco to start with, but as the other wolves joined us on the dance floor, I found a rhythm. Songs played and time passed. The dance floor got ever more crowded until we were all packed closely together. The tunes became sultrier. I raised my arms above my head, eyes closed, letting my form move with the verse and then the chorus. Vampires didn't sweat, but wolves did, and the scent pervaded my nostrils, more intoxicating than the alcohol.

Wolves began removing their clothes. Some just discarding shirts and tops as they grew hotter. Others peeling the layers away entirely. Lips locked and hips rocked. Some began to leave. I watched and I knew the three wolves were watching me watching the others.

"I'm going to get a beer," I shouted to Tommo. "I'm sober enough that I want another drink."

Tommo nodded over to where Kellan stood by the bar.

Fuck.

"He'll be the judge of that," he remarked.

I made my way off the dance floor and walked over to Kellan.

"Can I have a drink now Alpha Kellan? I've been a good girl," I said.

"Have you enjoyed the dancing?" he asked.

"Yes, once I got into the swing of things."

"And the evening in general. Have you enjoyed it?"

"It's been a lot of fun so far. Anyway, what's with the twenty questions? Can I have a drink or not?"

"I was checking you could hold a conversation before I made my decision. A beer for the lady please, Zariah."

"You should let loose yourself a little tonight, Kellan," I suggested.

"I'm in charge. The pack have the fun and I make sure they do."

"I'm in charge, so I'm going to be borrrriinng," I impersonated his voice the best I could.

"You can still be in charge from the dance floor, can't you? Anyway, some people are outside, and you're inside. It's impossible to watch everyone all the time. Your pack have a responsibility for themselves to mind their own safety and wellbeing."

"Quite the opinion you have there for someone who's been here all of three days and who isn't even a wolf."

"What-ev-er." I picked up my drink. "Thanks," I said.

"Do you want me to look after it while you dance?" Kellan asked.

"I'm not dancing now," I told him. "I'm going outside."

As I stepped away, he grabbed my wrist. "I'm not sure that's a good idea."

My eyes met his in a challenge.

"Then you'll have to come make sure I don't get in any danger," I teased. Pulling myself out of his grasp, I stalked towards the bar's exit.

I heard him mumble, "For fuck's sake," and his footsteps sounded out behind me.

Chapter 20

Kellan

I followed Snow outside. It seemed the woman was pushing her boundaries and exploring the edges of them to see if she could move further still. As the alpha, I had to ensure she was safe. As a male wolf, I was already feeling antsy about anyone touching her. Could Snow be like a wolf in her sexuality? Could she find her pleasure and then say thank you and leave it all behind her? I wasn't so sure. It was in a vampire's nature to become consumed by things, often to the point of obsession. To not be able to let it go. But she was a grown woman, and her father said only to make sure she was safe. He'd not asked me to stop her, and so I would do nothing but ensure that safety.

"If you're staying with me then I don't want to

hear your opinion about what I'm watching or what I'm doing," Snow said.

"As long as you're not in danger, it's not my concern," I stated.

"Really?" she probed, taking a mouthful of her beer. "Do you like to watch, Kellan? Do you watch the others when they share a woman?"

I startled.

"Pierce told me what they do," she elaborated. "It sounds incredible. Being worshipped all over, all at once. I do believe I might try it."

My nostrils flared. I couldn't help it. "I don't take part, and I don't watch," I gritted out.

"But if you're keeping an eye on me, you'd have to watch, wouldn't you?" She raised a brow.

I strongly wanted to drag her back to the bloody time out room, put her there, and call her father to remove her from the compound.

But I knew Snow was doing nothing wrong, even if she was teasing me mercilessly. That was the vampire way, was it not?

My problem was I wasn't sure if I could just watch.

After a moment's hesitation, I made a decision.

"Drink up, we're leaving," I ordered.

"I'm not going anywhere," she ground out. "You're not *my* alpha."

That was not the right thing to say to an already on-the-edge wolf. I grabbed her hair in a bunch and pulled her towards me. "I think you'll find while you're here, I am. Now listen up. You've made what you're wanting pretty clear, but I'm about to ask you to make it clear as a pane of glass. Do you want to make out or have sex with wolves tonight?"

Those dark eyes seemed like an eclipse in the moonlit sky.

"Yes."

I dropped my grip on her hair. "Which wolves?"

"The ones from the cabin."

"All of them?"

"If they want to join in."

"Fine. We will go ask them and then we'll go home. That's the only way this is happening, Snow. Though I've better things to do with my time, I will supervise you with the wolves."

"You don't need to supervise. I'll be fine with them. You trust them, don't you?" Before I could answer, she changed her stance. "Actually, no, you can't."

"What do you mean?"

"Until you find who murdered your father, you can't trust anyone. Not even the men you call brothers."

"Is that the conclusion of reviewing the evidence with Pierce? Trust no one?"

"Yes, you need to speak with him about it."

"And should I trust you?"

"I am trustworthy, but then even a villain would say that, wouldn't they?"

"They would."

"I accept your offer to watch. Let's go and collect the others. Just know that if you change your mind and wish to participate, my answer is yes."

I ignored her and began walking back inside to look for the others.

"It's very weird for you to ask the others to come back so I can fuck them," she said, as we were walking into the bar.

"I'm not asking them. I'm just not letting you out of my sight," I replied.

"You can keep up the 'I'm so cool' act if you like, but we both know you want to rip my clothes off my body right here and thrust your rock-hard dick inside me. Your control is admirable. I see how you're the alpha." Snow looked at me through heavy lidded eyes that swam with lust.

"And I now see the vampire in all her seductive glory."

"What do you mean?"

"The tease, the picturing of what might happen. What happens after you've milked their dicks, Snow? When the chase is done? Do these cravings of yours abate? Or do you crave more danger, more pain? I've never had such close contact with a female vampire before."

"We aren't the same, just like you and your wolves are different. We share commonalities, but my needs are not simply 'vampire' needs, they're *my* needs."

I wanted to continue the conversation, but we'd reached Ace and Samuel, who were leaning on the bar conversing and drinking. Their eyes lit up as Snow approached. "You enjoying yourself, Snowflake?" Samuel asked her.

"Yes... but I think I could enjoy myself more," she stated.

"How so?" Samuel asked, while Ace looked at my face, which despite my best efforts no doubt held a pinched expression. I was surprised my veins weren't visibly pulsing.

"If you're agreeable I'd like to invite you and Ace to come back to the cabin with me, to seek mutual pleasure," she said.

Their eyes widened and both looked at me.

"I will be there to supervise. This is Snow's decision, and yours. She wishes to invite you all to participate. Pierce spoke of how you sometimes share a woman and it's piqued her interest."

"I can speak for myself," Snow scolded.

"We'd be delighted," Ace said. "You're aware wolf sex is all about fun and satisfaction without the mate bond?"

"Fun and satisfaction is what I seek."

"I'll go speak to the others and we'll meet you back at the cabin," I told Snow.

"Thought you weren't leaving me..."

"I've changed my mind. Ace and Samuel can take you back. The rest of us won't be far behind you."

"Come on," Samuel said. "Let's have a stroll back so you can make sure this is definitely something you wish to pursue."

They left and I went to find the other three who were on the dance floor. I beckoned them over.

"Everything okay, Boss?" Tommo asked.

"Define okay. Is the pack fine? Absolutely. Everyone enjoying themselves? Seems that way. Does Snow want you all to fuck her. Yes she does."

The way Pierce's eyes lit up made me do something I wasn't proud of. "Pierce, I'm sorry but you've drawn the short straw. Someone still has to cover the security."

"But why me?"

"It has to be one of you."

"Why can't it be you?" he said. "Or are you taking part too?"

"I'm unwillingly keeping an eye on our guest while everyone else enjoys themselves," I stated. Snow will still be here tomorrow. If she wants a repeat, then you're in and Samuel will be on security."

"You say it like we're football players and one's on the bench. Can't Nala watch the cameras?" Pierce suggested. Then his expression changed to one of concern. "Oh, actually, no, scratch that. It's okay, I'll go do it."

"It's not Nala's place to cover, but why the change of heart?" I pressed.

He rubbed the back of his neck. "I was going to wait until tomorrow, but Snow came up with some theories. One of which is that Nala has good grounds to be the one who actually killed your father."

"What?"

"She knows the ways of vampires. She tried to stake Snow. Could be nothing, but..."

I pulled at my hair. This wasn't something I needed to hear right now.

"Go monitor the woods while the camp sleeps, and I'll see you later."

Pierce slunk off. The usually pleasant wolf was

decidedly pissed off right now. Did he suspect I'd chosen him because I felt Snow liked him the most? The fact that was the truth showed me my alpha traits were front and centre. Why didn't I just club Snow over the head and drag her to the cabin? Actually, knowing Snow, she'd enjoy that.

"I'll go and take his place if you want," Tommo offered.

I shook my head. "He'll do as he's bid. There's no contest between the security of our pack and sinking into some pussy. If he thinks there is then maybe he needs to rethink his position in my team. See, you've got the right idea, pack first. Let's go," I said.

"Always pack first," said Trent.

"Didn't hear you offer to take Pierce's place," Tommo sassed.

"Damn straight, but I wouldn't have argued with the boss if he'd asked. That's the difference."

"Pierce just has his first girl crush. His balls have finally dropped. If Snow's up for more then tomorrow we can show him what to do," Tommo said, laughing.

We set off towards the cabin, and for once I looked up to the sky.

If there is a God, please don't let this woman be our undoing, was my silent prayer.

Because there'd been no friction between us all before, but there certainly was tonight.

When we entered the cabin, Ace was taking blankets into the time out room. "I thought this room would be comfortable and private," he said.

I nodded.

"Samuel is getting condoms and a few other things. Snow is getting changed. She asked that you don't go up there to see if she's changed her mind. She said to tell you she hasn't," he said.

I pursed my lips.

"You okay, Boss?"

"It's just not something I thought I'd have to supervise this week. In the midst of everything else going on, this curve ball is something I could have done without."

"I see it differently," Ace said, quietly.

"Speak freely, Ace."

"Snow makes you different. I see a change in you when you're around her. Oh, I know she gets under your skin and annoys you, but she gets a response, Kellan. You show the rest of us what's not much more than a robot. Tonight is what, an hour at the most, because we'll go easy on her. Pierce is on watch. How about you do what we all know you want to do, and join in?"

The door opened and the others entered carrying more rugs and blankets. They placed everything so it looked as comfy as possible, and I saw the few sex toys that had been brought in slipped discreetly under the edge of a blanket.

A knock came to the door, and we watched as it opened and Snow walked in. She was dressed in the blue and yellow gown she'd worn for dinner, but where it had been laced in black before, this time it was threaded through with a red lace.

My rage spiked at her walking in here wearing something that she knew would remind me of the red ribbon. If it weren't in my possession, I'd bet she'd have walked in wearing the red ribbon in her hair. She was inciting me like I was a bull.

I got in her personal space. "Take. That. Out," I spat.

"If you don't like it, you remove it," she uttered. "I don't see why I can't wear my lace, or my hair ribbon. I haven't done anything."

"You haven't done anything? Look at us all, Snow. We're all being driven to distraction by you."

She sighed. "Okay, I'll remove it," she said, and for

one brief moment I thought I'd won. Until Snow pulled the long lace out. It all seemed to happen in slow motion. The bodice of her top separated, exposing plump, creamy breasts.

"You win, Snow, you win," I said, as I picked her up and threw her down upon the blankets. "You can tell us to stop at any time," I told her. "But you can't tell us what to do. We're going to show you what being with a wolf is like. Understand?"

"Yes." Snow looked around at all of us. "I can't wait."

Chapter 21

Snow

The pack didn't know how lucky they were to be able to be so free. They weren't judged for their playfighting, nor for the sex they treated as if it were just as important as food.

But who is putting these cuffs on you, Snow, I thought as I got ready. *Who is judging you?* And I realised, it was all me.

No one had told me I couldn't fight.

No one had said I had to limit myself to one person.

No one had looked at me and thought me a freak.

These were all judgements I'd placed on myself, used to being told Snow was pure. But it wasn't my family who'd said that to me. They'd said I was named for being beautiful and unique. They'd never said pure. It was the people outside of my family who uttered the words 'pure as snow'.

Here within the pack, I'd allowed myself to be my true self. Because here I'd freed myself of the judgement I felt would come from revealing my true self, even though I had no evidence it would.

I stared at myself in the mirror. Then I pulled out the black lace from Kellan's shoe, got my own red lace and rethreaded it. No more being anything but myself, I decided. I'd take a leaf out of Tommo's book, take me or leave me.

Then I went downstairs to experience everything the wolves had to give me.

I knew the red lace would piss Kellan off. I hoped he joined in. But as the lace was my choice, his participation was his.

Therefore, I was surprised, but delighted when he threw me among the blankets. I landed with a soft bounce, my breasts jiggling.

But Kellan didn't look at my chest. He looked firmly in my eyes.

"You can tell us to stop at any time," he stated.

"But you can't tell us what to do. We're going to show you what being with a wolf is like. Understand?"

"Yes." I looked at every wolf in turn. "I can't wait," I uttered, and it was the truth. Finally, I was being my true self.

The men gathered around me and shed their clothes. My eyes feasted on their naked flesh. At their muscled physiques: the washboard abs, beefy biceps, and hulking thighs. I took in Ace's clean-shaven face, and Tommo's dark stubble. They all were very different in appearance, but they shared one common denominator: a lust-fuelled gaze.

Samuel helped ease the dress off my body, until I was left in just my panties, and then Trent pulled those from my body too. "Wolves like to get naked," he whispered. I smiled.

Kellan hung back despite the fact he was part of the group. But the truth was, although I wanted him here, I wanted the others here just the same. My relationship with Kellan was different due to the circumstances that brought me to his pack, but in this room right now he was not the alpha, not to me. He was a wolf shifter and one of six men with an equal share in my body.

Diego laid next to me and pulled me towards him. His lips trailed down the slope of my neck in teasing little kisses that made my nipples bud. Their hardness was an accepted invitation from Tommo who moved in to capture a stiff peak. He sucked and laved and I felt it deep in my core.

Ace, who was down by my feet took a deep inhale. "She wants us, I can smell her desire," he announced.

Samuel and Trent picked up a foot each and began kissing the soles of my feet, working their way up until they reached my toes, which they sucked in turn. By now Kellan had taken my other breast and was teasing my nipple with his tongue. I was in sensory overload as Samuel and Trent moved up my calves, and Diego moved onto the other side of my neck. Ace kissed my stomach and lower abdomen. The need they were creating in me took me by surprise. I'd only ever had such a thirst for blood before. Not even the pain I sometimes sought compared to the craving within me now for these men to savour me; to bite, caress, coax me and claim me, even if only for tonight.

Then Ace dipped lower, settling between my thighs and flicking his tongue across my clit. I arched upwards and moaned deeply.

He broke off. "So responsive," he declared before delving back in.

Tommo left my breast and claimed my lips, his tongue seeking mine. While he did, a warm hand cupped the vacated breast as Diego's lips left my neck.

As Ace lapped at the juncture of my thighs, my eyes closed as I gave in to all the sensations that were happening to me all at once. A finger was placed on my clit, flicking, as the tongue penetrated my sopping wet flesh. My nipples were tweaked to a painful level, but I revelled in it. The storm was building inside me, whirling and gathering momentum, and as a finger slid down the crack of my butt and entered the hole back there, it was as if thunder shook my body, and lightning electrified my core. "Oh my God, Oh my God," I repeated.

"Oh, sweetheart. That was just the warm-up," Samuel teased. "Are you ready for us?"

I nodded.

Kellan moved to between my legs after putting on a condom, his rigid cock resting next to my warm heat. Ace placed one of my hands around his cock. Diego took my other hand and did the same. Samuel's dick rested beside my mouth. Trent and Tommo sat one either side of my body and began to trail feather light touches over my skin.

It was torturous in the best of ways.

Ace's hand covered my own and he began to move my hand up and down his shaft. Catching on, I did the same with Diego. I opened my mouth and accepted Samuel's cock, and then Kellan pushed inside me.

Trying to concentrate on everything at once was a challenge, but just like with the music at the bar, I soon found a rhythm. I moved my hands in time with the movements of my mouth, and let Kellan take the lead with fucking my pussy.

"That's it, baby," Samuel coaxed but his voice was getting gruffer, breathier.

Knowing he was close made me suck harder.

"Fuck, yeah, more," he encouraged.

Meanwhile Kellan had moved slowly in and out of my pussy, taking a leisurely pace, eyes closed as he pressed within me. The squelchy sounds made as he moved revealed just how turned on I was. How could I not be? I was in sensation overload.

Diego began working my hand faster around his dick, so I upped the pace with Ace too. Trent and Tommo's featherlight touches turned to more intense pressure as I began to beg. "Please, Kellan, I need to come again. Please…"

Kellan pulled out of me and for one horrified moment I thought he was going to leave, until I felt him return in a hard thrust, his pelvis grinding against mine.

"Yes. Fuck. Yes."

I forgot who was where as I closed my eyes once more, concentrating on creating pleasure and receiving it too. Ace removed my hand, and I opened my eyes to see him tug hard twice on his dick before he came all over my stomach. Diego followed suit a moment later. Samuel shot his load down my throat next. I greedily swallowed every drop, and then my attention was all on my pussy as Kellan picked up the pace thrusting within me over and over until I shrieked, convulsing around him and taking him with me. Kellan thrust a couple more times, and then withdrew, turning to deal with the condom. But it was still game on, as I was positioned onto my back. Trent climbed over my hips, pushed his fingers into my pussy, and lubed up my rear. Then he slowly pushed his dick in. "Just relax, Snow. It's okay if you can't take all of me yet."

'Yet' surprised me because it meant more. That maybe this wasn't a one and done, and that created an inferno within me. Relaxing as much as I could, Trent pushed in inch by inch. "That's it. Good girl."

Then Tommo moved from above my head. At first, I thought he was going to make me suck his dick, but he instead laid across my waist, placed his cock between my breasts, and then pushed them together.

"These juicy tits are ripe for fucking," he said, sliding his cock in and out of the channel created. He didn't give a shit about the other guys' cum, using it for lubrication.

As he slid back and forth, Diego took over one breast, Samuel the other, Kellan flicked my clit, and Ace plunged his finger in and out of me. The room was filled with grunts, groans, pleas to the lord, and slapping sounds.

Tommo came across my breasts and Trent finished in my butt, before they moved the others out of the way of my core. Trent licked my pussy while Tommo fired up a small vibrator, teasing my clit with it until I bucked all over Trent's mouth.

I flopped back against the covers basking in the sensations my body had enjoyed. I felt completely overwhelmed and like I was boneless.

"You bloomed under our touch, Snow," Diego asked. "Was it what you hoped for?"

"It was that and more," I said dreamily. "So much more."

"Have you had enough?" Ace asked. "We have toys you've yet to try."

I smiled dreamily. "Am I spent? Enjoyably so. Do I

have the energy for more? You bet I do. I'm a vampire. Takes more than that to tire me out, although I may go into an orgasm coma. Can't predict it as I've not been in this situation before."

"We'll monitor you for a potential orgasm coma," Kellan said with amusement.

"My turn to enjoy that sweet honey between your thighs," Ace declared, and it all began again.

Every one of them fucked me. Some with toys around their cocks that rubbed against my clit or vibrated. One shoved a butt plug in my arse while he fucked me. They cleaned up my skin of cum and then decorated me with it again. I sucked Diego's dick. It went on... and on... and on. Until Kellan called time.

"The sun will be coming up shortly," he said. "I'll take Snow up, get her washed and into bed. Anyone want to help?"

"I'll come with you," Trent offered.

I was tiring with the oncoming dawn and the antics that would have depleted the blood in my system. "Do you need a drink? An extra blood bottle? Diego asked.

I shook my head. "I'll be fine until the morning. But would someone kindly leave a bottle by my bedside, so I can have it on waking?"

Diego nodded.

Kellan lifted me and carried me over his shoulders. I was too tired to protest. Taken into the bathroom, the shower was put on by Trent, and as Kellan helped me stand upright, Trent washed every inch of my body in soapy water, before shampooing my hair.

He ran a brush through before Kellan told him he'd got it from here. Kellan helped me into my pyjamas and then rested against the headboard, pulling me between his knees, just as he had the time he fed me.

This time, however, he blow-dried my hair. "So soft," he said as his hands teased through it. "I could get you a different coloured ribbon?" he said gently.

I shook my head. "Thanks for the offer, but once I'm home, I can wear my red ribbon once more."

"That's true. So before you go to sleep, any regrets about the evening?"

"None," I said. "My father will be pleased to know you made sure I was happy."

He chuckled. "I'll let you in on a secret. For a short time there, I was happy too."

Kellan kissed the top of my head and then encouraged me to burrow down under the covers.

"Sweet dreams, Snow," he said. I was asleep before I knew what his own next actions were.

When I woke dusk was coming. Memories of the night before replayed in my head over and over. I was so very thirsty, and grateful to find the packet of blood next to my bed.

Once consumed, my lethargy fell away. Then once more all I could think about was that evening's adventures. I grabbed my journal as while it was fresh in my mind Ic wanted to record my thoughts and feelings of that night. I began to write…

The most amazing thing happened yesterday. Firstly, I ran with the wolves and the slower pace meant I felt my muscles were worked more. And then Kellan play fought with me. I could see the battle in his features as the guilt came about hurting me. I wish I could make him see that to me a fractured cheekbone is little more than a scratch. A broken arm a graze.

And afterwards? After, I slept with six of the wolves and it was glorious. The truth is, I've never felt like I belonged anywhere more than here with the Luna pack. I know it makes absolutely no sense. I am a vampire, not a wolf. But that's how I feel so that's what I'm writing down.

I cannot stay beyond Friday though. I must return home and look for a place that gives me what my time with the wolves has—the feeling of home. Yes, I have my loving home at Moonstone, but that's not my forever. I'm ready to move on to be the vampire I need to be, whatever that is!

Therefore, I must try to help the pack with this murder before I leave. Like I said to Pierce, if I track down the delivery drivers, I might be able to enthral them into telling me if they saw who dropped off the packages. It's worth a try. That reminds me, I have a question for my father. I'll be right back.

I sent a text to my dad.

Snow: How would a vampire or any other creature/person disguise their scent? Like there is no trace on the boxes Kellan has received of any other person beyond the pack and the delivery drivers. I wondered if there's a way of stripping that back and uncovering the murderer's smell?

My phone immediately rang.

"Snow, you need to talk to Kellan immediately," he said. No are you okay, no how are things at the compound.

"Oh? Why, what is it?"

"We can smell any scent, Snow. It's impossible to disguise it from a vampire's nose. Even just a low trace would be discernible to us, like if they washed the body in something like bleach to attempt to clean it and overwhelm it with the scent of chemicals. We'd still be able to smell what was underneath."

"The scent of death and decay was overwhelming," I stated.

"Either you've examined the body parts and missed a slight scent, or, and this is more likely, you have smelled all the scents. Which means…"

I gasped. "It is someone he knows."

"You need to find him immediately, Snow. I don't know how he'll work out who it is, but you're all in immediate danger. I know you don't want to hear this, but I want you to return to Moonstone now. You have to see this makes sense."

"Yeah, you're right. As soon as I've warned Kellan, I'll leave."

"Phone me as soon as you're home please."

"I will, Dad. Thank you. I love you."

"I love you too, dear daughter. If you need me then

call and I'll help the pack. Kellan already knows he can call me too."

"You're amazing. You do know that, right?"

"As are you. Stay safe and call me soon."

I looked back at my journal and quickly wrote.

Spoke with my dad who told me there would be a scent. They're impossible to disguise. The murderer has to be one of the pack unless I've missed a low scent. But who would do such a thing? I have to find Kellan and tell him. I need to re-examine the evidence.

A knock came to the door. I quickly stuffed the journal under the pillow. I opened the door to find Pierce at the other side.

"Hey," he said, smiling. "Just checking you're okay as you're late up. You've had your blood, right?"

I nodded. "I was just getting ready as I need to chat with Kellan about something."

"Oh yeah?"

"It's only about the meal tonight. Nothing important," I lied.

"My mum's downstairs. She's brought you some

flowers as a thank you for putting up with me," he said. "Can you spare five?"

"Sure," I replied. "What a lovely gesture. Just give me a second to change out of my pyjamas."

"Okay. See you down there."

I went to put on some clothes. I settled for my black sparkly leggings, and wandering over to Kellan's closet, I pulled out a plain black, long-sleeve t-shirt which hung on me like an oversized tunic. It wasn't ideal, but my t-shirt had a hole in it, my sparkly top had got ripped during the playfight, my white dress needed laundering, and my blue and yellow dress might bring back too many memories of last night if the wolves saw me in it again.

Then I went downstairs. However, the first thing I noticed wasn't a smiling mum with a bunch of flowers. It was the pungent aroma of garlic. Indeed, as I looked towards the sofa for his mother, there was no sign of her.

My confused state put me at a disadvantage as Pierce jumped out from behind me, holding back my arms. His mother appeared, forcing my mouth open and shoving a piece of garlic to the back of my throat. It burned. Oh how it burned. I coughed and my eyes streamed, blurring my vision, but I couldn't dislodge it. The pain was overwhelming and took the strength to fight away from me. I watched helplessly as a tourniquet was placed around my arm and Pierce began to draw the blood out of my body.

"Go make sure the coffin is ready now, Mother. I'll be with you shortly," he ordered.

Her eyes met mine and I thought I saw regret there, but with my vision clouded and being unable to concentrate, maybe I was just seeing what I wanted to see.

She left.

"I heard you talking to your father, Snow, when I first came upstairs. I'm afraid I just can't have you running off your mouth to Kellan. I have a pack to win over and an alpha to get rid of. Good job Mum was free to come help me deal with you." He ran a hand over my cheek. "Such a shame I didn't get to fuck you before I had to turn you into a wizened old husk."

Thank God I didn't sleep with him, I thought, but the relief must have been evident on my face.

"Fuck you," Pierce spat out. "For that look, you'll suffer."

He drew out more of my blood until I was too weak to do more than just lie there. Then he unfastened his trousers and freed his dick. I knew that the tears that escaped my eyes were not down to the garlic alone now. *Oh God, please no.* I mentally begged to lose consciousness.

Pierce thrust his dick inside my mouth hard.

"Great way to ensure that garlic is wedged perfectly in your throat," he said with a cackle. He withdrew his dick and reached into his pocket for more cloves. With a look of smug satisfaction and a sneer, he stuffed them in my mouth and then thrust his dick in again, making me baulk.

"That'll do. I don't want to dislodge it and ruin all the fun," he stated, taking his dick from my throat. He wrapped a hand around it and began jerking himself off. "Look at you, wearing Kellan's t-shirt like you're his woman. Poor, poor deluded Snow. Now my cum is going to pattern that top with my own snowflakes." He ejaculated all over the t-shirt.

"That's better," he declared, pulling up his pants and trousers.

I could feel my body growing weaker, while the pain from the garlic obliterated almost everything else.

Then the world blinked out.

Chapter 22

Kellan

I'd woken early and gone straight to the office. I'd sat amongst my father's things staring into space one minute, then been holding my head in my hands the next.

My brain was run ragged with thoughts. About all that had happened last night, and with the words Snow had uttered to me about not being able to trust any of my pack.

I had no one I could trust.

A knock came to the door.

"Yes?"

Nala entered. "Morning, Kellan."

"Nala."

"What time did you get here?" she enquired.

"I'm not sure, but early. Very early."

"After the run and the bar, I thought you might be in late. Shall I get you a coffee?"

I drummed my fingers on the desk. "Would you sit a moment, Nala?"

She frowned but sat down anyway.

"Snow reviewed the evidence yesterday. She didn't say much to me about it. Said Pierce would fill me in. She told me that I couldn't trust any of the pack. Not a single one."

"Why?"

"I've got to ask Pierce."

"So ask him. Get him here as soon as possible."

I hesitated. "The thing is, that Pierce also told me a little of Snow's appraisal of the evidence yesterday. She'd pointed out that you knew the ways of vampires well and could have made it seem like a vampire did it."

"And because I tried to stake her, that would add to the evidence against me, correct?" Nala looked weary.

"And you confessed to an argument with him before he left..."

"Kellan, are you accusing me of killing your father?"

I shook my head. "No."

"Then I don't understand."

I sighed. "I've spent hours trying to figure out why

anyone within the pack would want to murder my father and I just haven't been able to. But all I keep circling back to is that Snow told me I could trust no one, and Pierce told me I'd to be careful of you."

"I still don't understand where your train of thought is going on this."

"If I can't trust any of the pack, why did my top security guy only warn me of you?"

"Because I was the main suspect?"

I shrugged. "Could be, but there's something picking at my brain. I'm going to get him to come here, and while I do, I want you to be doing something for me."

"Yes?"

I passed her a small box containing labelled memory cards. "I want you to start with the day we found Snow beside the box and check the video footage during Pierce's watch. We were searching for a vampire before. This time look for anything unusual. If you find nothing, then go to his previous shift."

"You really think it could be him?"

"I'm starting with him and with Tommo."

"*Tommo!*" Nala exclaimed, her eyes widening.

"Tommo is ready to be named my deputy. He's been screwing Raina who I know would love to be the alpha's mate. She knows I'm not interested in her.

Maybe they're plotting my downfall so that he can take over the pack."

"Oh, Kellan. I'm so sorry that on top of losing your father, it looks like you have a snake in the grass," Nala said. "But I still don't understand why you've decided I'm innocent."

"Why? Are you guilty?"

"No, but the evidence still stacks up around me."

"Nala." I reached over and took her hand within my own which made her startle. However, she kept it there. "You sacrificed your happiness so that your son could be raised as a vampire. Then you fell in love with my father, and although you kept yourself at a distance from me, you also made sure I never wanted for anything. I've only been the alpha for a month and during that time I have realised just how much you supported him, and me. You just did it from behind your protective barrier, which I didn't notice because I was behind mine." I squeezed her hand. "I'm sorry I was too broken to see what an asset you were to my pack and what a wonderful wife you were to my father."

She began to weep. "I-I'm sorry that I couldn't let myself love you like a son, Kellan. But it would have seemed d-disloyal to the one I have."

I dropped her hand and embraced her. There was a newfound understanding between us now.

"Okay. Coffees, and then security check for you, Pierce for me," I said.

"You know where I am if needed," she replied.

"I do now, and I'm very grateful," I answered, meaning every word.

I called Pierce. "Hey, Pierce. How's Snow this morning?" I asked him.

"She's fine."

"Did she drink her blood?"

"She did. Snow's not mentioned anything about last night, but then seeing as I wasn't there, that doesn't surprise me. I've asked if she wants to go for a walk with me and she's just getting ready."

"Oh, okay. I was going to ask you to call by and give me the summary of what Snow had come up with regarding the evidence, but over the phone will have to do."

"It won't take long anyway. Snow looked over everything in detail. She couldn't detect any scent of an attacker. Her conclusions like I said were that the person you needed to be most suspicious of was Nala.

Please be careful, Boss. When I'm not on Snow-sitting duties, I'll do some digging around on Nala's movements and background. See what I can find."

"Thanks. Appreciated," I said, trying not to let any hint of suspicion about Pierce sink into my voice.

I ended the call, stood up and walked out of the office.

I stepped into Nala's. She looked up at me.

"Pierce said all Snow came up with was you. I know that's a lie. He says he and Snow are about to go out on a walk. What do I do, Nala? I've got Snow sitting with my potential enemy, but I've still no real proof."

"Say you've decided to go with them. That you need to clear your head," she suggested.

"Good thinking. Call me if you come up with anything."

"I will."

I sent Pierce a text.

Kellan: I'm going to join you. My head's a mess today. Could use the fresh air and your company.

But he didn't reply.

I took off at speed towards the cabin.

I entered the house to find Pierce sitting on the sofa looking annoyed.

"She's gone," he said simply.

"What do you mean, she's gone?" I shot out, my eyes darting outside as if I might see her.

"I don't know what happened. We were going to go for the walk and then she told me she'd decided to leave. She collected her backpack and went."

"And she's returning to Moonstone?"

"I don't think she is. I'm sorry, Kellan, but she said her night with the wolves was a huge mistake and she needed to get away. To disappear for a while as she felt shame."

"Fuck," I said, scrubbing a hand through my hair.

"Never mind Nala. Her father's going to want to kill you now," Pierce joked.

"I'd better call him," I said.

"I'm still going to go on the walk. My mum's coming now Snow isn't. Call me if you need me," he said, heading for the door.

But I was already on my way upstairs. I needed to see Snow's belongings gone with my own eyes. She'd seemed so sated last night, so happy. Why hadn't I been there when she'd woken up to check she was okay? Or one of the others who'd been there last night? Instead, I'd left Pierce.

You fucking idiot.

Walking into the bedroom, I could see all Snow's clothes were gone, along with her backpack.

"Fuck. Fuck. Fuck. Fuck. Fuck," I yelled. Rage shot through me. I punched the wall. I threw the lamp off the bedside table across the room, the ceramic base exploding. Even the scotch bottle became a victim of my anger and frustration. With the room turned almost upside down, I slumped onto the bed. Of course it smelled like Snow. Sitting up, I launched the pillow off the bed.

"Bloody woman getting in my head," I yelled.

But that was when I noticed the journal. It had been tucked underneath the pillow and it wasn't locked. Without a second's hesitation, I opened it and began reading.

It was all there.

How happy she'd been last night.

How she'd told Pierce she could try to enthral the delivery drivers.

How she was going to warn me about the lack of scent and re-examining the evidence.

But she'd not.

And now Pierce had told me she'd left as she felt shame.

It was a complete and utter lie.

So where was she?

My phone rang. The display saying Nala.

"Hello?"

"I've found something. Earlier, on the day you found Snow, Pierce's mum Angela walks into the woods on her own with a picnic hamper. She disappears out of view and although she reappears with the hamper, she doesn't sit and enjoy a picnic. It wouldn't have caught my attention, other than the fact that it's close to where you found Snow... and the box."

"I need you to gather the others and tell them what we talked about this morning and what you've discovered. Snow is missing. Pierce has told me she left of her own choosing, but I've found her journal, and she had no plans to go. He's gone for a walk. I can only hope he's not staked her, or my own life is over, Nala. Beau Salinger will not let me live if I didn't keep his daughter on this earth."

"So what are you going to do?"

"I'm going to call Beau and then I'm going to Pierce's mother's house as he says she's gone on the walk with him. Maybe she's involved."

"I'll send all the council to you, and I'll cover the cameras. You need your team, right now, Kellan. Your family."

"Thank you." I hesitated. "I count you in that, Nala. You're my family too."

"Let's make your father proud," she said. "By kicking wolf arse, and let's not think the worst unless it's confirmed."

"Easier said than done," I noted.

"I know, but if she is still out there, Snow needs you at your best. Keep me informed."

"I will," I agreed, and then I ended the call.

"Beau," was all I had to say.

"If she is not safe, Kellan Luna…"

"She's missing. I think one of my own is my father's murderer and he's responsible for Snow's disappearance."

"Missing or staked?" Beau said slowly as if he was fighting the words leaving his mouth.

I took a deep breath. "I honestly don't know."

"I'll be with you within minutes, Kellan, after I talk to my wife, so be waiting to open that fucking front door."

I walked downstairs and left the door ajar and then I paced the room. The next I knew, my head was ricocheting off the back wall.

Slumped on the ground, I looked up at the crimson eyed vampire. This was Ella's father. I thought of what she'd said about being afraid of him being a father, rather than a vampire, and I saw that beneath his need to obliterate me, was heartbreak.

I got back to my feet. "I have a lead. We need to visit Angela Luna's house. My wolves are being updated as we speak and will meet us there. At the end of all this, if you wish to beat me within an inch of my life or drain me dry, I will not put up a fight. But for now, we need to work together to find her."

"The house then," he said, and he ran there with me.

There was no sign of anyone home. Beau tore the front door off its hinges, and we went inside. I took my time, but Beau flew around the room, belongings being strewn everywhere. He thrust a pile of photographs and letters in my hand. "Start there," he said, and he disappeared off into another room.

I sat looking through the photos. There was

Angela at a younger age with her family. Her wedding pictures. Photos of Pierce. Then in a well-handled envelope was a picture of my father. He was laid asleep in a bed. But it wasn't any bed I recognised. I felt ice cold dread in the bottom of my stomach, and I knew that if I walked upstairs, I'd see exactly which bed he was laid in.

There was nothing else of note, other than that one photo, but I knew it held the answer to why all this was happening. Beau walked back into the room. His face solemn.

"Anything?" he said.

I held up the photo. "This is my father. Asleep in a bed I don't recognise."

Beau walked over to me and knelt by my side. "It's Angela's bedroom, Kellan. I've just been in there."

"I thought as much," I sighed.

Beau placed a hand on my back. "I found something else, Kellan. I'm so very sorry."

"What?" I asked, my heart thumping in my chest. If the man whose daughter had disappeared in my care was looking at me with sympathy then this was something major.

"My sense of smell led me to the cellar. Your father's body has been separated into many parts and is being kept in a freezer down there," he said softly.

Chapter 23

Beau

It had been difficult enough for my wife to accept our daughter needed time to be alone. But Ella had given in to my demands and we'd had a lovely first couple of days at the Lakes. Wrapped in my arms, she'd confided in me as to how she felt Snow wasn't being honest with us about something. That our daughter often seemed out of sorts.

I agreed. It was why I'd encouraged Snow to think about a small trip outside of the castle while she had the chance.

I'd already argued against us leaving to collect Snow, and maintained she should be allowed to stay with the wolves as was her choice.

Now I had to tell Ella our daughter might be no more.

I couldn't bear it.

I loved Ella and my children more than words could describe. But to try, it was like they lay within my heart cavity and filled it with love. Sometimes I felt it so strongly I imagined my chest could burst open. Now I had to find my wife and tell her something no parent ever wanted to hear.

Her scream could no doubt have been heard from space.

"Beau. No. Not my Snow. I refuse to believe it. She must be out there somewhere. If he's killed her… I will tear his skin from him one layer at a time. I won't kill him. I will keep him in eternal damnation."

I called for Isabel and Dove and had to explain to them too about their missing sister, and to ask them to care for their mother while I was gone, and to help her inform the younger ones of what was happening.

"I will turn over the earth to find her," I said. My solemn vow.

I kissed them all on the cheek and then left.

Now I sat next to the man whose bones I'd wanted to break and told him I'd found his father.

He sat in perfect stillness, the photo he'd held now laid on the floor beside him.

Kellan closed his eyes for a second and then he climbed to his feet.

"We need to find Snow."

"And Pierce and Angela."

"Snow is the priority, but I'm guessing where we find Snow we'll find them," I said.

We heard voices then and the others walked inside. Kellan did the introductions. "Trent, Ace, Diego, Samuel, and Tommo, this is Beau, Snow's father."

Ace stepped forward with a hand outstretched. It trembled though as it hung there. "Sorry about the circumstances in which we meet, Sir. We are very fond of Snow."

My eyes narrowed as I looked him over. Had this man grown close to my daughter? Is that why he'd stepped forward first?

"Yes, we are all very fond of her," the wolf called Tommo stated, holding out his hand too. One by one all five said variations of the same thing and shook my hand.

"I can't believe it. Not Pierce," Diego uttered. "We all grew up together."

There was a silence then while they waited for

further details or instruction. But their alpha was staring into space.

"I located your prior alpha, Kellan's father," I told the other five wolf shifters.

Audible gasps sounded out.

"Where?" Tommo asked.

"There's a freezer downstairs in the cellar," I stated, letting them work the rest out for themselves.

"Fuck, Kellan, I'm so sorry," Trent said, taking a step forward to embrace him. But Kellan didn't respond to the man's actions. He just went into business mode.

"My father's not going anywhere. We leave here now and try to find Snow." He turned to me. "Your scenting skills will be invaluable right now. How shall we proceed?"

"I will go through your woods first. If you might come with me to direct me to where you first found my daughter…"

"Of course."

"What about us?" Tommo asked. "Do we tell Nala?"

Kellan shook his head. "No, I will do that. I want you all to go through this house and turn it completely upside down to see if there are any more clues here. Tommo, please arrange to transfer my father's body to our funeral parlour. It won't be an easy task to see him like that, I know, but someone has to do it, and as my deputy-to-be, I'm assigning it to you."

Tommo nodded. "You got it."

With everyone given their instructions, Kellan and I made our way out of the house. "Tell Nala," I instructed Kellan. "You don't want her hearing it from anyone else."

"But we need to find Snow."

"I'll go to the woods now. You don't need to be a long time. Just give her the facts."

He sucked on his top lip contemplating.

"You're right. I will be minutes, Beau. I'll come meet you in the woods."

He sprinted off in the direction of where Nala must be, and I whizzed into the woods.

But there was no evidence of my beautiful daughter.

I'd never felt turmoil like it. I fell to my knees and cried in pain.

Chapter 24

Kellan

"Kellan!" Nala exclaimed, and then her whole body slumped at my hung expression. "You've found him."

I nodded, and pulled Nala's other office chair forward, sitting in it. I wheeled myself so I was facing her and took hold of her hands.

"He's in Angela Luna's cellar. In the freezer."

Nala broke down and sobbed. I gave her a minute, and then I had to interrupt. "I'm sorry to leave you but I have to go to the woods to meet Beau and start our search for Snow."

She sniffled. "I understand."

But my phone rang, and Beau informed me that there was no trace of Snow in our woods. That he would return to Angela's house to see if the wolves had found anything that could give us a clue as to where she might have been taken.

After the call ended, I rubbed at my eyes.

"I know you don't believe, Kellan, but I'd like to use my crystal ball," Nala said. "You can leave and meet Beau if you wish, but I want to see what it says."

"I'll stay," I said, feeling Nala needed my support in this moment and Beau would call me again if he needed me in the meantime.

Nala took the crystal ball from a drawer in her sideboard and switched it on. She turned and looked at me hesitantly, as if embarrassed to speak to it in front of me.

"Go on," I prodded.

She swallowed and began.

"Oh, crystal ball, I need to know,
If the alpha's true mate is the vampire Snow.
And where it is she might be found.
We seek reassurance she is safe and sound."

Colours swirled inside the ball, and then a voice began to speak.

"Your alpha's mate is not safe or sound,
But lies imprisoned upon higher ground.
Her fate relies on being found,
And having her father and wolves around."

I thought it had finished, but it went on.

"If you reach her in time, fate will challenge you all.
Question is, will you answer the call?
The alpha's mate is not his alone.
There's a test to everything you've ever known."

Then the swirls in the ball cleared and showed us a glass coffin, on a mountainside surrounded by trees and topped with snow.

But where was it?

"I'm off to Angela's house to meet the others," I declared.

"I'll come with you," Nala stood.

I was about to refuse her, but she folded her arms across her chest.

"I'm going to help bring my husband back here," she insisted.

"Fine. Let's go," I stated, and we left the office building to return to Angela's. On the way I told Nala of the photo I'd found.

"But wouldn't he have been married to your mother then?" she queried. "It makes no sense. Your father loved your mother dearly."

"We might never know," I said. "But you can be damn sure I'll try everything to find out."

As we approached the house, Beau came out to greet us. "We've found the deeds to a small cabin in Aradale. It's worth exploring."

As soon as he said it, I knew that's where Snow was. It was a village set in the valley of a small mountain range. I'd bet that's what we'd seen in the ball.

But as I was about to tell Beau about the crystal ball's information, suddenly, his mouth opened in a snarl and a hiss, his nostrils flared, and he was gone in his full red eyed glory.

"What the fuck?" I said to Nala.

We looked in the direction of where he'd darted, and I was debating if I should set off in pursuit when Beau returned, his hand around Angela Luna's throat. "Time for questioning," he said, and I followed him inside the house.

"I c-can explain," Angela said, choking against Beau's hold.

He threw her down onto the living room sofa and sat at her side. "If you attempt to escape, you'll be dead before your body finishes rising from the sofa," he warned, in a tone that could have frozen the air inside the house. Angela's chin trembled and the smell of urine seeped from her.

I got a dining room chair and sat in front of her.

"Is Snow in Aradale?" I asked.

Angela didn't speak.

"Why is my father's body in a freezer in your basement?"

Still nothing.

Beau whipped her up off the sofa and explored her pockets, unearthing her mobile phone. "I'll get Pierce back here, shall I, and you can watch as I tear him into the exact same pieces more or less as you cut Santos into." He began swiping her phone.

"No! Okay, okay, I'll speak," she said, seeming to collapse in on herself. "But I want your vow that you won't kill my son, Kellan. Punish him, jail him, but please don't kill him. Let me be able to visit him wherever he is. It's why I've done everything I can to protect him. A mother's love. And also... you wouldn't kill your own kin, would you?"

"What are you talking about?" I asked, my patience wearing thin.

"Pierce. He's your brother," she said.

I stared at Angela. "Quit with the bullshit and tell me why you've my father's murdered remains in your basement."

"I need your vow," she said again.

"Kellan won't kill him," Beau added, his eyes meeting mine sending a blatant message of who would.

I knew as pack alpha it was my role to end the life of a murderer. It would usually be done in front of the pack adults to set an example, but I doubted I'd get near Pierce anyway. Angela wasn't thinking straight bearing in mind she was sat at the side of Snow's father. Though I wanted my vengeance, I'd seen enough blood and body parts without being responsible for the same. Now I was focused on Snow. On getting her back. Making sure she was safe. I wouldn't think past that.

"Why do you have a photograph where my father is lying in your bed?" I asked.

Angela's look became wistful. "Before your father bonded with your mother, I was his favourite lover," she said. "We spent a lot of time together. Years altogether. But as soon as he met your mother, he was gone. I missed him so much, but he'd left me with something precious. I was pregnant."

I gasped. Was she actually telling the truth?

"As you know, it's extremely rare for an unbonded pair to create a child. It's also nigh on impossible to separate a bonded couple. I threw myself into sleeping with more of the pack and met Riggs, who convinced me he'd felt the mate bond. I didn't bond back, which in itself would have been unusual if not for the fact that Riggs was a liar and hadn't bonded with me at all. I told him I was pregnant, and we got married. Pierce was born and Riggs took him on as his." She paused to take a breath.

"Go on."

"Riggs told me later that he smelled I was with cub when he met me and that's why he married me. His mother had been hounding him to continue the family line. Riggs continued to fuck around while we played at happy families. He never asked who Pierce's real father was because he didn't care. We had our own cubs a couple of years later, our two sons and daughter and that was the most settled I ever saw him. He appeared a true family man then and we were happy. Yet as soon as his mother died, he left the pack. Said the kids were old enough to cope without him and he wanted to escape the confines of mothers, wives, and fatherdom and enjoy himself. I was devastated because although we'd not bonded, I deeply loved him.

"Santos came to see me one afternoon to check how I was. He was there in only his capacity as alpha, but he spent time asking me about my children and if I needed anything from the pack now their father had left. He'd heard Pierce was becoming unruly and wanted to know if I needed him to have a word with him. Pierce was cheeking teachers, playing truant from school, and stealing. I was feeling vulnerable, and I told him the truth. That Pierce was his son. I don't know what I expected to happen, but it wasn't for him to get drunk and beg me to keep our son a secret. You'd been born within a year of Pierce's birth and news of a secret child would rock the pack. As he was older than you, Pierce would become your father's heir. Santos didn't want your mother to know. Didn't want your place usurped. I understood."

Beau held up a hand. "You okay, Kellan? Need a minute?"

I shook my head. "Every extra minute is a minute without Snow. Continue," I ordered Angela.

"Your father went upstairs to use the bathroom and I later found him asleep in my bed. I took a photo. It was only for me. Not for blackmail or any other salubrious reason. I just wanted a memento of the man I loved. I woke him up. He was embarrassed at his drunken actions and couldn't wait to leave. Santos promised to keep an eye on Pierce from a distance. He said he would encourage Kellan to befriend him. Santos said he would watch over him as a guardian, but the truth could never be known."

"Unbeknown to me, Pierce had truanted school again that day and had climbed into his bedroom through the window. He walked out to find us leaving my bedroom. He assumed we were lovers on an afternoon tryst and assumed that was why his father had really left. That he'd discovered my affair."

She closed her eyes and took a deep breath. "The night your mother died; the night you were with her, Pierce had come back with cuts and bruises. He told me he'd hotwired a car and was driving around when he'd spotted Santos' car. Rage had fuelled him to chase it. The car had lost control trying to escape the pursuit and had crashed into a tree. He didn't know it was your mother driving and you were inside."

I felt like a car had hit me, right here, right now. Pierce had caused the crash that killed my mother?

Injured me? All because he thought my father had caused his own father to leave?"

"He swore it was an accident. That he'd never meant to hurt your mother or you, and I believed him. I told him I'd not been having an affair with Santos, and he was mistaken. That he'd called in to check on us on his way home, had been drunk and had fallen asleep on his way back from the loo. Pierce listened but to my own ears it sounded like a lie, even though it was the truth."

"I need you to speed things up now because my daughter is out there with him," Beau ordered. "What happened that meant Santos ended up in your freezer?"

"You did befriend Pierce," she said, looking at me sadly. "And as you both grew older, Santos gave him a place on the council where he flourished. I was so proud of him and thankful to you and your father for setting him back on the right path. Santos was proud of him too and just before his death he came to see me again to tell me that although he couldn't acknowledge his son publicly, we'd created something amazing. He thanked me for keeping my secrets. What I didn't know was my son, the head of security, had my house covertly under surveillance. I'd rebuffed him fitting the house with security cameras, so he'd fitted ones I wouldn't notice. He'd done it for my safety, but instead found out the truth.

"The next morning Pierce called me in a panic. He knew Santos ran every morning and he'd followed him. He'd told Santos that he would need to declare him his son officially and make him his alpha-in-waiting. Santos had tried to reason with him, but his insistence Pierce keep quiet made him lose his temper and kill him. Pierce said the fact I'd lied about there never having been an affair meant I owed him. That this was all my fault. We put him in the freezer and Pierce decided he would make out as if there was a vampire enemy who'd killed him. When Snow showed up, he couldn't believe his luck. Pierce had intended on leaving a box there that night, to convince you the enemy had found a way to enter the compound. But with Snow present, he blanked out the cameras and left her there, thinking you'd kill her and that would be the end of it. Then we could dispose of Santos' remains in due course."

"But I didn't kill her."

Angela shook her head. "That tipped him over the edge. He went into a rage and said he would make sure you looked inept. His latest idea was to frame Nala which would knock your confidence further. Though Pierce was older than you, Santos' death meant you'd automatically become the alpha. Therefore, the only way Pierce could now take your place would be to challenge you. That was his plan. To create a lack of confidence in your leadership and to then say I'd confessed at his being Santos' child. Then he'd take over the pack."

"And you felt no guilt at covering for him?"

Angela began to cry. "I didn't know what to do. He's my son, and I did him wrong. I lied to him for years. I'm partly responsible for his behaviour."

"You're a fool," Beau snarled. "Your son is a psychopath. He's not suffering childhood trauma because his father fucked off. You think your lies caused him to be responsible for two murders?"

"The first was an accident," she protested.

"And you're sure of that are you?" Beau pushed. "Pierce would have been happy to stand by and watch as Kellan killed my daughter because she just happened to have been in the vicinity. All so he could continue with his twisted games to become the alpha of the pack himself. The place he believes he deserves as the oldest of Santos' children."

Angela was sobbing hysterically now. We had the truth, and it was time to deal with Pierce once and for all and to rescue Snow. But we needed to confirm where she was.

"Is Pierce holding my daughter in this Aradale place you have the lease for?" Beau pressed.

Angela nodded. "I was going to retire out there. My sister lives there. I recently bought it so I could visit on weekends and pretty the place up. When Pierce phoned me and said he needed my help to capture Snow, that she was getting too close to the truth about who'd killed Santos, I suggested we take her there."

Beau pressed on Angela's windpipe then loosened his touch a little, getting into her face. "What did your son do to my daughter in order to capture her and take her to Aradale?"

"H-he just bled her so she was powerless," she said, but even I could see her lies. Beau's fangs descended. "I suggest you tell me the truth because my patience with you and your son is thinner than the finest layer of ice."

"I-I made him change her into a pretty dress. I went out and bought it in Aradale." Angela hung her head. "Because when I arrived, I found him urinating on her t-shirt. He'd already come on it too, he said."

"I suggest you tell me my daughter's exact whereabouts right this second, and if I find out he's done more to my daughter than you've said, I will make him eat his own cut off penis in front of you."

"He hasn't. He promised. Pierce was just showing

his superiority. Snow's in the mountains, laid in a glass coffin. It was Pierce's plan to give you her safe return in exchange for his life. I was coming to see you, Kellan, to tell you, but you were already here."

"Bullshit." I slammed my hand down hard on the floor. "You'd no idea we were here. That we'd found my father. The only reason Snow is alive is because you didn't know if she might still prove useful. Pierce has no idea we know of his guilt." A thought hit me. "Is he waiting for the all clear from you?"

Angela's guilty face answered the question.

"Pass me the phone, Beau. I will text Pierce. I'll look at her previous messages and see how she usually answers. I'll tell him everything is fine, and that I've accused Nala and put her in the time out room."

"And are we done questioning Angela?" Beau asked, passing me her phone.

"We're completely done with Angela," I said.

Her eyes went wide. "Wh-what? Don't hurt me, please. I can help you get your daughter back."

Beau's face would have frightened the devil himself. His eyes were as dark as autumn maple leaves and his lips, as pale as his skin, were fixed in a grimace due to his canines and his fury.

"Your son was willing to sacrifice my daughter's life

to save his own, and you have left him alone with her. Your words are worthless."

He disappeared out of the room dragging her by the throat and shortly after we heard a gut-wrenching scream sound out from the cellar.

Next, I heard the kitchen sink running, before Beau returned. He held up a bowl filled with blood. "Angela said she'd help get my daughter back. She was right. Do you have some bottles I can use? Her blood can help replenish my daughter. I think that's quite fitting in the circumstances, don't you? he said.

Chapter 25

Kellan

I sent the text to Pierce and Beau went off to find his daughter. The pack would join him once we had Pierce at the cabin.

For now, we had to act as if nothing were amiss. I told Nala my plan and then we returned to the cabin. Nala stepped into the cell Snow had been in, and I took my place across from her. The others in the room stayed near the door, so that once Pierce came in, he had no chance of escape.

Then we waited. Pierce wasn't long. The temptation to see Nala in the cell and to convince me she was guilty was too much for him.

He strolled in wearing a look of condescension and shook his head in Nala's direction. "How could you think you'd get away with it?" he accused.

"Indeed, that's my own question," I said, and that's when Pierce noticed everyone else's expressions.

"What are you talking about?" His eyes went to the exit, but he'd no chance of escape. It was him versus seven other wolves. Nala's cell door wasn't locked.

"We know you killed my father," I said simply.

"My mother did it. I've been covering for her," he shot out. "She was Santos' lover."

Even now, he was willing to throw his mother under the bus to save his own skin.

"That's not what your mother said... just before she died."

For a brief moment, shock flooded Pierce's body, and then his anger rose. He turned into his wolf and so did we.

I didn't kill him. I kept to my word. Instead, I spoke to the pack telepathically and we held him down while Nala came forth and ripped out his throat. Pierce had killed her husband, and he'd been willing to let her die for it. She looked at me as blood dripped from her mouth.

Thank you, she uttered through the mind link.

We're going to Snow, I told her. *Use my bathroom to clean up, and leave Pierce's body here. We'll deal with it on our return. Gather the pack and update them on everything.*

I will, she stated.

And then as a united pack, my brothers and I set off for Aradale.

We found Snow still laid in the glass coffin, Beau weeping at her side. "The blood's not enough, Kellan. She took it, and her body has lost its gauntness, but still she lies there. I've also given her as much as I can of my own, but it's not enough. I've never seen a body so drained. Pierce had shoved garlic in her throat too. Tons of it." His voice cracked. "She must have been in so much pain."

We all gathered around the coffin. It was actually a glass box, possibly from a shop. I'd hazard a guess it came from the same place as the dress she wore had. I'd bet that was where the ribbon and boxes had come from too. In the long, plain black dress, Snow looked paler than ever. The fact black was funereal made my heart clatter in my chest.

And as I faced the chance that Snow was beyond recovery, I realised I loved her.

"You can't leave us, Snow. I won't let you," I yelled,

frustration taking over. Without delay, I ripped open my wrist and let the blood pour into Snow's mouth until I was weak and dizzy from it.

Beau pulled me away. "That's enough, Kellan."

I stared at Snow. Her lips had naturally lapped and took in the fluid, but she lay still once more. In turn, Tommo, Ace, Diego, Trent, and Samuel followed my lead and fed her until they were depleted, and Beau pulled them away. As each wolf gave her their blood, Snow's capillaries began to show beneath that pale skin until as Samuel finished his donation, her cheeks bloomed, and she opened her eyes.

Snow looked around at us all and then noticed where she lay. The hand her father had been clutching gripped him and she sat up. "Where am I?" she asked in a panic.

That feeling I'd had. The one like a curled-up snake, hit me hard and I keeled over clutching my stomach, only to find the other wolves doing the same. Then emotion burst out of me in a roar, as I turned into my wolf. Five other wolves roaring and rippling around me.

All of us looked at Snow and bowed our heads.

We'd mate bonded with a vampire woman. Every one of us.

Chapter 26

Snow

The last thing I'd remembered was passing out in Pierce's company. Now I awoke, feeling too weak to open my eyes, barely aware of the blood being fed to me. But as if buried alive and scrambling at the earth to find the surface, eventually I had the strength to open my eyes.

Immediately, I'd seen my father, then the wolves. Fear hit me as I saw I was in a strange place, in a strange dress, and sat in a glass box. For a moment, I was distracted as the men around me all turned into wolves and then stilled at the side of me with bowed heads.

I looked at my father. "What's happening? I don't understand."

"They've bonded with you, Snow. All six of them."

"What?"

"Don't think of it right now. Let's just get you home. Your recovery and regular feeds are what you need, and your mother and siblings will not rest until you are safely in your own bed in the castle."

My father turned to Kellan.

"I know you have bonded. But you have your pack business to deal with and I am taking Snow home. We will speak later, Kellan. I cannot thank you enough for what you've all done. You've brought my daughter back to me."

Kellan nodded.

"I would be grateful if you could leave us now. I've been left quite weak and I'm going to contact my wife and other children to come with more blood. I don't think it's a good idea for you to meet Ella under the current circumstances."

The wolves rose and ran out of the area. I felt a small pang in my chest, but then exhaustion overtook me again. My father contacted my mother, and soon my family were by my side. They brought blood and as I drank my absolute fill, soon I was physically able to go home, though my father insisted on carrying me back regardless.

The moment we were through the door of Moonstone castle, my mum took over. "Let's get that disgusting outfit they gave you from your body," she ordered, "and we'll have you in a nice cleansing bath. Then I insist on the doctor coming to examine you, Snow. We don't know what that man did to you while you were unconscious."

I thought of how Pierce had thrust his penis into my mouth. Weak, pathetic bastard. I was just thankful I hadn't slept with him, and I would have done. The man had fooled me completely.

As my mother helped me bathe, it reminded me of how Kellan and Trent had cared for me after we'd slept together.

"Mum, can I tell you everything?" I asked. "Even if you find some of it uncomfortable?"

"Of course, you can, sweet daughter." She stroked my cheek, and I let everything out: my seeking of pain, my sleeping with the pack, what Pierce had done to me.

"Even more reason for the doctor to check you over. While there will be no evidence of injury there could be evidence of semen."

I cried then and prayed that Pierce had not subjected me to that.

Thankfully, the doctor found no evidence and while it was still possible Pierce could have done it, I doubted it. I was sure he would have wanted to look me in the eyes while he attacked me in such a way.

For the next twenty-four hours my family kept close to my side, and while I felt perfectly recovered physically, mentally I still had a lot to process.

The wolves had bonded with me.

What would they think about that? Would they try to find a way to undo it? The Luna pack could not continue with a vampire woman as its alpha's mate, could it? Bearing in mind she'd also be the mate of the rest of the council. And what about children? They wouldn't be pure wolf.

It was too much for me to think about and I was pleased when dawn broke and I could fade away from my thoughts.

Chapter 27

Kellan

I instructed my pack by the mind link that we would return to the compound, and we ran from the mountainside, leaving Snow behind. Every step away from her sent a pang into my heart and I knew the rest of the pack would feel the same way. But, just as Beau had said, we had pack business to deal with right now. And Snow needed time to recover and to think. As a vampire, we would receive no mate bond in return, and as a pack what would that mean for the future? It was too much to contemplate. As alpha, my role now was to clear up the mess left by Pierce and his mother, reassure my pack, and bury my father.

We discuss Snow tonight. Our attention right now is on clean up and council duties. Clear? I told the others.

Clear, I received back from all.

As soon as we emerged from the woods and entered the main area, we ducked home to get new clothes, given ours had been left in Aradale after we changed. Then as Tommo supervised the start of removing Pierce's body, I caught up with Nala.

"How goes it?" I asked, walking into the office.

"Kellan!" Nala stood up and threw herself at me, wrapping me in a large hug. "Thank goodness. How is Snow? Tell me everything." She realised she was hugging me, let go, and stepped back. "Well, screw it all," she exclaimed. "Seems I've grown fond of you anyway, despite my best intentions to keep my heart locked away."

"Likewise." I grinned. "Pesky emotions, eh? All six of us wolves realised we loved Snow, and mate bonded with her. Outrageous."

Nala's mouth dropped open. "You did *what?*"

"Mate bonded. Fell in love. The whole shebang."

"I think you'd better tell me everything. Right from the beginning," Nala ordered.

I was happy to, because I still couldn't quite believe it myself.

"And now what? How does that work?"

"You tell me." I shrugged. "I'm going to talk to my

brothers about it tonight, but Snow might not wish to see us again or ever step foot back with the Luna pack. We're giving her space and time with her family. How were the pack when you told them about Pierce?"

"Extremely shocked about Pierce and Angela. I think it will take some getting used to that we had an enemy within. They need their alpha."

"And that's my focus, right now. Let's get Pierce and Angela's bodies dealt with and then hold my father's funeral tomorrow. Then we'll have the official ceremony for my becoming the alpha in two days' time on the full moon with a huge party afterwards. Other than that, all we can do is let time pass and our pack heal."

"Got it. What do you want me to do next?" she said, and we began to call people and make arrangements.

That night, the pack gathered around to hear me speak about Pierce and Angela.

"No one was more surprised than me to find out the murderer of my father was Pierce Luna. However, there is some further information I wish to share with you all. It was brought to my attention that Pierce was my father's son. He and Angela having conceived the child shortly before he mate-bonded with my mother.

"It in no way excuses Pierce's behaviour. He killed

my mother. Then he murdered my father. He tried to frame Snow Salinger and then Nala Luna. I shall wonder why my father didn't confide in me for the rest of my days, but in all other ways he was an incredible alpha. Always there to support you all. Tomorrow we will celebrate his life and officially mourn his passing.

"But let this be a lesson to anyone who would wish to make an enemy of our pack. Pierce did not succeed."

Angela and Pierce's bodies were brought out in front of everyone. How they were killed clear to all. They were placed on the ground in front of me.

"Angela and Pierce are expelled from the Luna pack. Their bodies will be taken to the woodland in the mountains of Aradale which they were so fond of and will be left for the wild animals there. Anyone who wishes to say their goodbyes, do so now."

Some did say words of sorrow, others spat, swore, and kicked at the bodies. Then they were bundled into shrouds and Tommo and Ace left for Aradale.

"We will gather here again tomorrow for my father's burial. If any of you feel he's no longer worth your respect because of the secret he kept, then please do not attend. For his faults, he was my beloved father and our beloved alpha, and he will be treated with the uppermost reverence."

With those words, I dismissed everyone, and went home.

You wouldn't have known anything untoward had happened in the time out room. I knew one thing though. After keeping Snow in there and then Pierce being killed in there, it needed redecorating. As did Pierce's room. While memories would remain, some DIY and a coat of paint or two would help with a fresh start.

I texted Beau.

Kellan: How is Snow?

Beau: Very quiet. Enjoying being in the closeness of family. How are you all?

Kellan: Banishment ceremony done. My father's burial tomorrow. My and the council's official ceremony the day after that. Then we shall celebrate the full moon.

Beau: Where you and the other wolves will crave my daughter.

Kellan: In time your daughter will decide where she wants to be. If it's not with us, we shall

find ways to cope until the mate bond realises it's not been acknowledged.

Beau: How can a wolf mate bond work with a vampire?

Kellan: I've been considering this. Vampires have fated mates, do you not? It is not so different from the mate bond. I believe us wolves may recognise it as the same. In any case, we will find a way if Snow wishes to be with us.

Beau: Be patient. My daughter just needs time. But I feel I know where her heart belongs.

Kellan: I bet you wish it didn't.

Beau: I told you before that I just wanted my daughter to find the kind of love where a man would give up his life for her. I watched you feed her, and I know that if it had come to sacrificing your life, giving her every drop, you would have done. All of you. I had to tear each of you away from her.

Kellan: I love your daughter. We all love your daughter.

Beau: Something I'm mentally trying not to think about as a father. But I shall think of you tomorrow as you bury your own. I am sorry for your loss. Good evening, Kellan.

. . .

I placed my phone down and waited for my fellow pack brothers to return.

Finally, we were all gathered on the sofas. After talking over everything that had happened, we were all in agreement that we hoped Snow would return.

"I'd like to completely renovate the house," I said, having decided that a small redecoration wasn't enough. "Get in architects and make a separate time-out space. Re-design the interior so it suits six wolves and their mate. Everyone needs their own room, but we also require a playroom."

"And a room where Snow can throw herself around if she needs it," Diego suggested. "Like her own jungle gym. Just in case she doesn't want to exhaust herself with us."

"Do you think she'll return?" Samuel asked. "My chest hurts because she's not here."

We all agreed we were suffering from her distance.

"I hope so," I replied. I couldn't say anything more. Like Beau had said, we had to be patient.

My father's burial took place the following day. Nala threaded her arm through mine, and we walked behind the wooden coffin that held his body—all of it.

Fond words were spoken, goodbyes given, and then we drank beer and wine as his coffin was set alight on a pyre. His ashes would be buried in the Luna mausoleum.

It had been a busy couple of days and by the time I got home that night, emotions and beer had me passing out the moment my head hit the pillow.

Chapter 28

Snow

Two days had passed. I'd woken feeling much more myself, but my head swam with confused thoughts. I wanted my family, but I missed the wolves. Craved their nearness. Wanted their comfort. But I also had this feeling in my gut. My usual craving for pain was filled with a need to hurt myself to get Pierce out of me. I'd not been able to fight him in real life, and my body and mind felt to me like his imprint was still there; his dirty cum invisibly tattooed on my flesh. I messaged Andre.

Snow: Are you free? Usual place?

Andre: Hey stranger. Thought you'd fallen out with me.

Snow: I went away for a few days.
Andre: Thirty minutes?
Snow: See you then.

I got ready and went downstairs.

"I'm meeting Andre," I told my mother.

"Oh honey. Are you okay?" she asked.

"It's like he's inside me. Pierce. And I need him out," I confessed.

"And fighting will help with that?"

"Yes."

"Very well, but Phillipe will accompany you," she stated.

"No," I protested. But I looked at my mum's face and knew it wouldn't do me any good.

"He'll stay out of the way, but I'm sending him with you. He understands more than you know, Snow. Talk to him."

Phillipe joined me in the hallway shortly afterwards. "Have you used your journal?" he asked me.

"I did. But I left it behind with the wolves."

"Well, if you don't return there, I'll get you another," he said. "I find mine helpful."

"You journal?" My voice gave away my surprise.

"Yes, and I fight. Just the same as you. It's normal

for us, Snow. I knew you were going out and meeting Andre. I turned up to the building once and saw you there. There's a few of us use that old derelict building. The difference is, I talked to dad about it when I felt running wasn't alleviating my instincts. He told me some vampires needed more and suggesting I boxed with other vamps. That's how I discovered the old school building and free fighting."

"Why didn't you challenge me?"

"Because it wasn't my business. But it's why I gave you the journal. I was trying to hint that I knew, and also give you an outlet for your thoughts."

I hugged him. "I love you, Pip. Come on, let's go fight."

"You mean watch you fight."

I shook my head. "The wolves playfight each other. Why can't we?" I said. "Bet you I wipe the floor with you."

"Only if I let you win because you're a girl," he teased.

Andre was surprised when we both turned up at the old school building. In fact, his mouth twisted in disappointment.

It made it clearer than ever that Andre wanted more from me than I could give him. Tonight, would be the last time I called on him. It wasn't fair.

"Andre," Phillipe said, holding up a hand to high five. Then as Andre went to meet it, Phillipe swung his other arm round and punched him in the ear.

"Phillipe!" I shouted, shocked.

"Such a girl," he said. That was it. I launched at him and soon punches and kicks were raining down everywhere between the three of us.

And with no guilt about any of it, I found it glorious.

"Come on, Snow. Pretend I'm him, the dickhead. Hit me," my brother encouraged. Andre was unaware of any of what had happened, but he picked up the thread.

"And me. Let it all out," he urged.

I did. I allowed my rage to come out knowing this was a safe space and my brother and friend could not be hurt by anything I did.

When we were finished, we all sat down resting against the wall.

"What's been happening then, Snow?" Andre

asked.

"Want me to step outside?" Phillipe asked.

"If you don't mind, Pip," I asked.

"I mind you calling me Pip," he complained.

"I can change it to Pipsqueak if you prefer?" I joshed.

With a roll of his eyes, he left Andre and I alone.

"Did you find a fuck buddy who proved to be a jerk?" Andre asked. Jealousy caused his eyes to flash red.

I shook my head. "No. I got kidnapped, and attacked," I stated.

Andre leapt to his feet and his fangs descended. But then the most shocking thing happened. His red eyes flashed yellow.

Wolf yellow.

"Erm, Andre," I said. "I think you'd better calm down."

"Who did it?" he rasped.

"They're dead. It's all over. It's a long story, but you deserve to hear it. You've been my friend for a long time. Please, please, come and sit back down," I pleaded.

"Friend," he said sullenly, sitting back beside me and returning to his usual eye colour of brown.

I told him of the wolves, of my attack, and finally I

told him that I'd fallen in love with them. All of them.

"My mother was a wolf," Andre said, looking at the floor. "My father drove her away. He wanted to pretend I was a full vampire. But I'm not. Something he clearly couldn't get past because he had many other full vampire children with other women, and slowly forgot about my existence."

"I'm so sorry, Andre. I just assumed you'd moved out from your family home." I felt guilt hit then that I'd never really asked Andre about himself yet had called upon him so much when I needed to fight. I sucked as a friend and now vowed to do better. "Do you know who she is?" I asked.

"I know her name and that if I searched, I'd find her, as all carry their pack name. But if she wanted me, she'd have come looking for me, wouldn't she?"

"I don't know how she'd feel about you making contact, but don't you at least want to try?" I queried. "If she turns you away, at least you'd know for sure."

"I'm too scared. I'm not sure I could face her rejection," Andre confessed.

"I'll go with you," I told him. "You've done so much for me, that it's the least I can do. We can go now. What pack is your mother from?"

"All I know is her name is Nala Luna," he said.

For a moment I couldn't find my speech.

"Oh my fucking god." My hands flew over my mouth.

"What? Snow, what is it, you're scaring me."

"I know where she is, Andre. Your mother is the widow of the wolf pack I stayed with."

"You've met my mum?"

I nodded. I didn't add that she'd tried to stake me. So Nala had an estranged son. Well now it was time for her to explain why she'd seemingly abandoned him, and it was time for me to support my friend. I realised then that I would see the wolves and heat began to build in my body. The urge to see them was one I could no longer resist.

"Do you know what else, Andre? I want to go tell my lovers that I love them. That I want to be with them. There's no time like the present. Come on, let's go," I said, climbing to my feet and holding out a hand for Andre.

"You won't abandon me for your lovers if she tells me to fuck off?"

"Never," I promised, and he reached for my hand.

Outside, Phillipe turned to me. "Heard it all. I'll tell everyone. Good luck, both of you," he said.

After hugging my brother, I turned to Andre and smiled.

"Let's go."

Chapter 29

Kellan

The ceremony started at five pm. We'd all dressed in our finest suits. I was as nervous as a groom on his wedding day and looked like one too. After everything that had happened of late, part of me still expected a protest, like that point in a wedding where they ask if anyone objects.

I looked out over the gathered pack, at everyone waiting for me to be officially declared the alpha.

And then we were underway.

There was a protocol to the ceremony. First, three of the oldest pack members stood and gave readings of the Luna pack's history and values. Next, Ace's father —who had agreed to conduct the ceremony—took me through my official declaration.

"Kellan Santos Luna. You are officially inaugurated as Alpha of the Luna pack," he announced to a mighty round of cheers and applause.

What followed then was my naming of my team. Everyone kept the role they'd served for my father, except Tommo, who I announced as my deputy. Finally, I named Marnie Luna as Tommo's replacement, and Annie Luna as the new security member of the pack. It was time for this pack to make changes and adding some females to the team was the first of many. Nala, as alpha mates before her, would become an advisor to the council, able to help where needed, but also able to relax if she so wished. She'd worked at my father's side for years and now could take a slower pace. Though knowing Nala she wouldn't.

With the ceremony complete, my deputy announced that the celebrations would begin. Everyone made their way over to the bar to start an evening of drinking, dancing, and no doubt debauchery.

I felt happy as I looked at my pack and vowed to make them proud of me. But I couldn't help the empty feeling I had that Snow wasn't there, taking her place as the alpha's mate. Maybe one day she'd make her way back.

I thought I was having an hallucination as I

spotted her walking towards me. She was dressed in jeans and a loose green sweater, her hair in a high ponytail. The only problem was, she was accompanied by a male vampire. One who did not look younger than her, and so therefore was not one of her brothers.

Swallowing the growl caught in my throat, I did my best to smile at Snow. By now, the others were approaching, and so was Nala.

Nala and Snow had not been in each other's vicinity since the staking, so I wasn't sure this was such a good idea.

"Snow, I want to apologise," Nala said, but Snow held up a hand.

"Later, Nala. There's something more important. I have someone who wishes to speak with you. Your son."

"A-Andre?" Nala croaked out, her voice breaking with emotion.

The vampire looked unsure but nodded. "I'm Snow's friend. She suggested I come to introduce myself and see if you'll answer some of my—"

He didn't get a chance to finish as Nala swept him up into her arms. "My son, my son. Oh my god. How? How is this possible? Have you been nearby all this time?"

Son? This was Nala's missing son? The very vampire Snow had been fighting with?

"Andre, do you want me to stay with you?" Snow asked him, her tone firm.

"I promise you he's in safe hands," Nala said. "Although I understand your caution."

"I'm okay," Andre told Snow. "You have your own matters to discuss."

"But I said I would support you. So are you sure? Don't say you're okay if it's just so I can talk to the wolves. My priority right now is you."

Once more I had to swallow a growl. I was also clenching my fists so hard my nails were digging into my palms.

"Honestly, I'm fine, Snow. I'm ready to spend some time talking to my mum, and I'd rather do it in private, if that's okay?" he said, looking at Snow like he might offend her.

Snow deliberated and then her shoulders relaxed. "Can you make sure he gets home safely, Nala? Unless of course he chooses to stay," Snow asked her. By doing so she gave an indication of trust to my stepmother.

"Of course. Snow, you've brought me my son. I will be eternally grateful." With tears in her eyes, Nala looked at me, smiled, and then stepped away, directing Andre to a seated part of the bar.

"So what does a woman have to do to get a drink around here?" Snow sassed. "Six hunky wolves who declared me their mate and yet I'm stood empty handed."

Tommo guffawed and stepped towards the bar.

"Are you back, Snow?" Ace questioned her.

"I missed you and I wanted to be here," she said. "And I wanted to let you all know..." She left us hanging until Tommo returned with her drink. "...I love you all too."

We drank, we danced, and then we ran into the woods. Snow sat and watched the playfighting having told us how she, Andre, and her brother had already exhausted that part of each other before coming here.

My eyes and a couple of the others had flashed with yellow at Andre's name and Snow had laughed. "I'm yours, you morons. I can't believe you're acting jealous, and you'd better get used to Andre as I think he'll be around here quite a bit from now on."

"You're ours." Samuel sighed with happiness.

It approached midnight. "Tonight, the moon changes us, Snow. Run with us?" he asked.

"Of course," she said. "Then afterwards shall we head back home?"

Home. She called it home.

Now we *all* sighed with happiness.

Chapter 30

Snow

I was exactly where I needed to be. With my wolves. I was so proud of Kellan becoming the alpha officially. I was just sad to have missed the ceremony. My head turned towards Andre who was still chatting away with Nala. He caught my gaze and gave me a huge smile and a thumbs up. I was so happy for him.

At one minute to midnight, I itched with anticipation at the fact the pack were about to become their wolves, and then I started to feel a shiver. My body rippled and I gasped as fur began to force its way through my skin. The other wolves all stood stock still. Then Andre came running over, his eyes the amber of his wolf.

"Snow. You're a wolf," he declared.

If I could have spoken, the word, 'Duh', would have come out.

To be honest we're all as flabbergasted as Andre is. Kellan's voice came through my mind.

How on earth can I be a wolf? I thought back.

How about we don't worry about that right now, and instead, come run with us, just in case it doesn't last long, Trent prompted.

He was right. And while I could there was something else I wanted to do. Something other wolves were doing.

I howled at the moon.

My wolves joined in with me, and then we ran, bursting through the trees. Nala and Andre ran alongside us and others from the pack joined in.

I had absolutely no idea what had caused this, but I was going to make the most of it while it lasted.

I'm taking Andre back to the bar, Nala said through the mind link.

Can everyone speak to me this way, and hear my thoughts? I asked her.

No. You can speak freely just as you would with your mouth. But your inner thoughts are your own. Only your mates can talk to you without being present. Anyway, I know what's coming next and so I think it's best Andre doesn't watch. He knows you belong to the wolves, but his crush still needs to recede.

What's coming next? I asked her.

You, Snow, Nala said.

Her and Andre left, and I looked around me. Wolves had made their ways to various places in the woods, and me and my six lovers did the same.

My wolves prowled around me, sniffing at me and making cute noises. Instinct kicked in and I moved my tail to the side to show them I was willing to mate. One by one they mounted me, and I enjoyed sex in this most raw and natural of ways, as my wolf. As our climaxes approached, each wolf bit down on my neck causing my body to react like I'd never known before. Pleasure ricocheted through me and I howled in unison with the wolf. As I laid down with my wolves laid around me, I knew I could never leave them now.

They were mine. All mine.

A pain shot from my abdomen, rising and growing in feeling and bursting free in a form of complete and utter joy.

I'd bonded, as a wolf, with all of them.

And they recognised it, all roaring in delight.

We rolled around together in celebration, and I bit every one of their necks, sealing the union.

Then I changed back into my human form, the others following suit.

"You're my mates," I stated, beaming.

"And you're ours," they said back.

Lust for my mates as a bonded female sent me dizzy. "I need you all," I begged. "In me. I need your cum inside me."

Kellan's brow creased. "Do you know what you are saying, little Bambi? Your wolf legs are still wobbly. Perhaps think on it some more."

"No," I snapped back firmly. "I don't need to think on it. We're together now. I'm all in. And if you are, then I want you, *all* of you. I want to birth your cubs. Let someone's seed take hold."

I could tell Kellan still worried, and the others looked to their alpha, even though as lovers they were his equal.

"I need it more than I need pain, Kellan. Does that make my position on things clear?" I asked.

"You itch for it, for our cum, deep within you? You're ready to swell with our cubs?" Ace checked.

"I burn for you all. The need so great, I feel I might die," I stated dramatically.

"Well, thank goodness you're already dead," Trent joked.

"Wolves usually have multiple cubs as you know,"

Tommo stated. "If you have all our cum in you, more than one of us could father them at the same time."

"You mean like if I carried triplets, I could have a baby Tommo, a baby Ace, and a baby Trent?" I queried.

"Exactly, ooh a baby Trent," Trent declared.

"No one needs another Trent. Get a condom on him," Samuel quipped.

Question time was over, and my wolves shared me, passing me between them. Entering me from behind, from in front, and coming within me over and over, as I myself shattered around their cocks milking them for every last drop. None of them asked me to suck their dicks and I knew why. But I didn't want Pierce here in our sex life. Poised over Tommo, I lifted his shaft and placed it near my mouth.

"You don't have to do this, Snow," Tommo said.

"I do, but can the others hold me?" I asked.

At first, as I took Tommo into my mouth, I felt a salty tear slide down my face as the unwelcome image of Pierce came into my mind. Strong, warm arms enveloped me, and my lovers peppered kisses over my body. Soon my bad memory faded away and new memories were made as I watched Tommo's eyes shine with lust, heard his groans as he approached climax, felt those strong arms supporting me through this moment. I knew it would take time, that the assault from Pierce would always linger, but at least it wasn't stopping me from giving myself fully to my lovers.

I pleasured all of them in turn, pleased that due to being a vampire, my achy jaw soon healed itself for me to start all over again. By the end of the evening, every one of my lovers cum swam within me. I'd never felt such happiness as I did now, wrapped within their arms.

Samuel lifted me up. "Let's not risk falling asleep out here in the woods," he said. "Let's take you home."

"Yes," I agreed, happily. "Take me home."

Chapter 31

Snow

This time I'd slept in Trent's bedroom. I woke to find him sitting in a chair nearby watching the TV.

"Hey," he said. "Thirsty?"

I nodded and he passed me a bottle of blood.

"I called your father last night to let him know you were staying with us."

I raised a brow. "And how was that received?"

"Your mother took the phone off him and said that every one of us was to visit Moonstone castle tonight for dinner."

"More like for an interrogation," I mused.

"Anyhow, I got your father back on the phone and explained how you'd changed into a wolf. He thinks it's because you were so depleted. As the amount of wolf blood you were given was so vast, being much more than the vampire blood your father donated, you seem to have been re-set as part wolf."

"So vampires don't have to worry that if they drink from a rabbit they'll grow whiskers and a cute fluffy bunny tail?"

Trent laughed. "Not unless it's actually a psycho were-bunny that drinks them into almost desiccation and then reanimates them."

I smiled again, but it had reminded me just how close I'd come to not existing anymore. One small stake in my withered state and I'd have blown away in the breeze.

"Did my father think I might turn again?" I queried.

"We've actually bet on it. I say you'll change every time we run through the woods, and your dad says it'll just be on a full moon. So," he encouraged. "How rested are you?"

"It's not even that you want my body, is it Trent?" I scoffed playfully. "You just want me to go running so you can potentially win a bet."

"I will always want your body," Trent replied. "But can we run first?"

"Get me my trainers." I shook my head at him. "By

the way, where are the others?" The house sounded quiet.

"Council business. They'll be back for dinner," he said, throwing a trainer at me.

Shortly afterwards, Trent won his bet.

Chapter 32

Kellan

"I'm sorry to call everyone together here with such short notice," I addressed my pack who I'd called out to a meeting urgently. "But I have an issue to discuss of the utmost importance."

They sat quietly and waited.

"Ace, Diego, Trent, Samuel, Tommo and I have all mate bonded with Snow Salinger."

There were some gasps of shock.

"Following Snow's attack, we gave her our blood to feed her and due to a reaction from being near death, she has become a hybrid of wolf and vampire. Last night she changed into a wolf and mate bonded with us too."

"I saw her. Her fur was beautiful. Jet black and so

soft," Raina said loudly. For once I didn't mind the woman's overbearingness.

"The Luna pack welcomes those of mixed species," I said. "Including Nala's son, Andre." Eyes flitted to the vampire sitting amongst us. He'd gone home before dawn but had returned again today to get to know his mother better.

I placed a severe look on my face. "I'm aware that some will follow the old ways of purity and not wish to deviate from them. If you wish to leave the pack, there will be no ill will from any of us. Anyone who stays will need to recognise Snow as not only the alpha's mate, but also that of the other five wolves. For those of you that do choose to leave, please come say goodbye to me officially, and where I can, I will help you to begin somewhere new."

With my speech over and everyone dismissed, I made my way over to Nala and Andre. "Do I have someone who may wish to join the pack?" I enquired.

"I have my own place right now," Andre said. "But maybe one day."

Nala smiled at that.

Chapter 33

SNOW

We all sat around Moonstone's large family dining table. My father had been the perfect polite host, while my mother supervised Gene cooking dinner. He wanted to learn how to entertain wolves, he'd said, in case he got a wolf girlfriend. My mum had rolled her eyes hard, but told me that it got her out of all the prep.

Every one of my wolves had taken my mother's hand and raised it to their lips, whispering polite words of introduction and stating how beautiful our home was. Charmers. She had however, cornered me in the kitchen and told me she could see why I didn't want to come home anymore.

Now dinner was served and we all sat together, my

siblings weaved within the wolves in the seating arrangements.

"So you're all Snow's husbands?" Reid asked. "How's that work?"

Trent sniggered.

My mother gave him a pointed look.

I addressed Reid. "Because of the mate bond, which is a feeling of love, it counts as marriage in a wolf's world. We will however have an official ceremony at some point. The wolf pack love to party."

"Will I meet wolves around my age?" Gene asked.

My mum rolled her eyes again knowing he meant girls.

My father noticed Isabel kept looking at her lap.

"What's so fascinating on your skirt, Isabel?" he questioned.

My sister's face flushed and she brought up a book. "Sorry. It's just so good."

"Isabel Mary Salinger, at least you will live with your father for the rest of your days, given that your head will be too busy in a book to notice a suitor."

"I'm sorry," she said again, looking around at everyone. "It's just sometimes once I start reading, I can't stop."

"I'm the same with my PlayStation but I don't bring it to dinner," Reid argued.

"I know a man who owns the biggest home library you've ever seen and yet hasn't ever read a single book," Diego told us.

"Is he human or supernatural?" Dove asked.

"He's clearly an idiot," Isabel answered before Diego could. "I may visit him to ask if he would like to donate all his books to me. There's plenty of room at Moonstone for them if he doesn't want them," she said.

"You will not go to a complete stranger's house alone," Mum insisted. "Look what happened when Snow went out."

"She's sat here happy with her six husbands," Isabel argued. "I could sit happy with all that guy's books."

The conversation moved on, but I saw the curiosity weaved on my sister's face. Who would have a house full of books and never read one? Isabel would not understand that and would not be able to resist the draw of increasing her own library, plus the mystery more interesting than any book.

I would need to tell Dove and Phillipe to keep a close eye on our sister.

Because the guy might be a gentleman, or he could be a beast.

THE END

Author note: If you enjoyed Snow, please leave a review!

They help so much. Going forward, I'm not using pre-orders until the book is written in draft form, so for updates on Isabel's book please sign up to my newsletter:

geni.us/andiemlongparanormal

About Andie

Andie M. Long is author of the popular Supernatural Dating Agency series amongst many others.

She lives in Sheffield with her long-suffering partner and son.

When not being partner, mother, or writer, she can usually be found scrolling TikTok, at her allotment, or walking her whippet, Bella.

She's addicted to coffee, Toblerone, and vampires.

Andie also writes contemporary romance as Angel Devlin and psychological suspense as Andrea M. Long.

About Andie

Stay in Touch!

Andie's Reader Hangout on Facebook

www.facebook.com/groups/haloandhornshangout

Instagram and TikTok:
@andieandangelbooks

Website
(store under construction)

www.andiemlongwriter.com

Paranormal Romance By Andie M. Long

PARANORMAL ROMANTIC COMEDY TITLES

SUPERNATURAL DATING AGENCY

The Vampire wants a Wife
A Devil of a Date
Hate, Date, or Mate
Here for the Seer
Didn't Sea it Coming
Phwoar and Peace
Acting Cupid
Cupid Fools
Dead and Breakfast
A Fae worse than Death

Paranormal Romance By Andie M. Long

Also on audio, paperback, and a series bundles available.

THE PARANORMALS

Hex Factor
Heavy Souls
We Wolf Rock You
Satyrday Night Fever

Also in paperback. Complete series ebook available.

SUCKING DEAD

Suck My Life – available on audio.
My Vampire Boyfriend Sucks – available on audio.
Sucking Hell – available on audio.
1-3 audio collection now available.
Suck it Up
Hot as Suck
Just my Suck
Too Many Sucks

Sucking Nightmare
Good Suck with the Wedding

PARANORMAL ROMANCE TITLES

DARK AND TWISTED FAIRY TALES

Caging Ella
Sharing Snow

STANDALONE TITLES

Filthy Rich Vampires – Reverse Harem
Royal Rebellion (Last Rites/First Rules duet) – Time Travel Young Adult Fantasy
Immortal Bite – Gothic romance

Printed in Great Britain
by Amazon

44098777R00212